OF VAMPIRES & GENTLEMEN

Borgo Press Books by A. R. MORLAN

The Amulet: A Novel of Horror
*The Chimera and the Shadowfox Griefer and Other Curious
    People*
Dark Journey: A Novel of Horror
Ewerton Death Trip: A Walk Through the Dark Side of Town
*The Fold-O-Rama Wars at the Blue Moon Roach Motel and
    Other Colorful Tales of Transformation and Tattoos*
Of Vampires & Gentlemen: Tales of Erotic Horror
'Rillas and Other Science Fiction Stories

OF VAMPIRES
& GENTLEMEN

TALES OF EROTIC HORROR

A. R. MORLAN

THE BORGO PRESS

MMXII

OF VAMPIRES & GENTLEMEN

FIRST EDITION

Published by Wildside Press LLC

www.wildsidebooks.com

DEDICATION

To the memory of

ARDATH MAYHAR
(1930-2012)

I can never repay you for all the help you gave
me by restarting my publishing career, but I
hope this volume is at least some justification
of all your efforts on my behalf.

I miss you, dear friend....

CONTENTS

ACKNOWLEDGMENTS

"Duet on Thin Ice" was first published in *Night Terrors*, Issue #4, 1997. Copyright © 1997, 2012 by A. R. Morlan.

"Initial Appeal" (the basis for the published story, "Dear D.B. ..."), is published here in this form for the first time. Copyright © 2012 by A. R. Morlan.

"Mother Gothel and Persinette" was first published in *Symphonie's Gift*, #3, 1995. Copyright © 1995, 2012 by A. R. Morlan.

"Little Nips" was first published in *Symphonie's Gift*, #2, 1995. Copyright © 1995, 2012 by A. R. Morlan.

"Of Vampires and Gentlemen...." was first published in *Prisoners of the Night*, #1, 1987. Copyright © 1987, 2012 by A. R. Morlan.

"...And the Horses Hiss at Midnight" was first published in *Love in Vein: Twenty Original Tales of Vampiric Erotica*, edited by Poppy Z. Brite, HarperPrism, 1994. Copyright © 1994, 2012 by A. R. Morlan.

"The Uppyroake Kamikaze and the Virgin Shredder" is published here for the first time. Copyright © 2012 by A. R. Morlan.

"Dark Ladonna" was first published in *Crimson*, #14, 2000. Copyright © 2000, 2012 by A. R. Morlan.

"At Funland, by the Swings, with Big Chuck" was first published in *Red Eft*, Vol. 2, Issue #1, Fall, 1997. Copyright © 1997, 2012 by A. R. Morlan.

"Yet Another Poisoned Apple for the Fairy Princess" was first

FOREWORD

Ever since I was a child, people have been either telling my mother, or telling me directly, that I was something of a "dark" person—not physically (I'm about as white-bread as a human can get: light hair, light eyes, beyond pale skin), but emotionally. I've never been the happy-go-lucky sunny type, and this has often caused those around me to fret and cluck and tsk-tsk about my gloomy outlook on life...as if *my* way of being somehow affects *their* ability to enjoy life.

Personally, I simply go with my own somewhat stagnant interior flow—as a certain spinach-eating cartoon character so aptly put it, "I yam what I yam." But my unique way of seeing the world often affects my work; while I have created some softer, more positive works, the bulk of my fictional output is... *dark*. Some works more so than others.

The stories here are among (but certainly not all) my darkest creations; some are sexually disturbing, others visceral and graphically violent, while others are (here I go with that *word* again!) just plain dark in nature. While I wouldn't go so far as to call them erotic, a few do have elements of the erotic in them. But I doubt most folks would get off on them!

I've also included three of my vampire stories—literally the first one I wrote, followed by what has been undoubtedly the most successful one (both financially and in terms of it being named as one of the *Year's Best Fantasy and Horror* stories in that long-running anthology series), and concluding with a previously unpublished story which just happens to be the last vampire story I've decided to write—in order to show my personal evolution in that sub-genre. As you'll see, I don't do dreamy romantic vampires, and they certainly aren't suitable for nine-to-twelve-year-olds and up...not that I think that the cleaner, "vegan" vampires, aren't just as worthwhile or as literary as what I've done with the sub-genre. I give all those writers my greatest respect—make it any way you can, and give the people what they want, just as long as people are picking up a book or a Kindle® or a whatnot and actually *reading*.... I do feel pretty certain that what *I* consider a vampire story wouldn't appeal to the fans of the "nice" vampires, but I'm not offended by that—literature needs to appeal to varied tastes; if *all* works of fiction appealed to *everyone* equally, I think we'd be in trouble as a species!

Now that I'm done with my personal rant, on to the stories....

A. R. Morlan
2012

DUET ON THIN ICE

Unseasonably soft and mild, the fitful southwest breeze ruffled the thinning oiled hair which the Reverend Alredge Merewode had so carefully combed across the crown of his head, threatening with each errant gust to reveal the tonsure-shaped bald spot which the cleric strove to conceal whilst among his fellows at the University, but— "And thanks to the All Mighty," he whispered through lips rough-chapped and just slightly numb from the half hour or so he'd spent skating the sun-sheened surface of Loch Coventina—since he was currently the only living soul within sight or hearing occupying the immediate area on this late December afternoon, the Reverend found no need to stop his daily exercise in order to secure his neck-scarf over his almost-unveiled pate. That such an act would have suggested a most unseemly show of vanity was not a concern of the good Reverend—ever since his hair began to thin during his days in the seminary, Alredge unconsciously began to use his remaining locks as a form of natural camouflage for Nature's tonsorial stinginess— rather, Reverend Merewode was instead concerned about the cutting-short of his time spent gliding across the lake's frigid winter flesh.

Framed from the casual prying eye by a monk's fringe of larch and pine, Loch Coventina was off-set by a quarter mile from any road or path, so that on its opaque whiteness, Alredge Merewode could guiltlessly cast off his mantle of clerical obligations to his fellow clerics and students, even as he surrendered his albeit lumpy and ungraceful earthly self to the momentum-driven *snniiiccckkk* and *shhhuuussshh* of his blades gliding across the glistening cold ice. Borne across and around the ice on curled-toe skates, he could surrender himself to the cold, to the relentless forward motion, to the grayish-greenish-bluish blur of the surrounding trees and distant mountains—and to the keening undulation of the wind rushing through the needle-burdened branches, the frost-stiffened rushes and reeds surrounding the loch.

The crisp, sustained *whoosh* and *shwoosh* of each blade's journey across the ice (the sharp metal just barely incising a trail on the hoarfrost behind) formed a soothing counterpoint to the susurration of the wind, one which eased the lines of worry from Merewode's typically furrowed brow, and one which allowed him to exchange the downward turn of his parched lips for a slight but mentally significant upward arc...until the cleric noticed that the wind's erratic counterpoint was a counterpoint no longer.

Rather, it echoed the whole-note-long one-foot-then-the-other forward rhythm of his skating; when he allowed himself to slow down to a stand-still on the ice, close to a rigid bristling of sun-whitened and wind-bent dead reeds near the southern-most shore of the loch, the strange counterpoint-that-was-no-more also ceased.

"Yet the breeze still blows...almost warm upon the flesh," Merewode muttered, his exhaled breath nearly invisible thanks to the uncharacteristic gentleness of the wind. And, when he paused to truly listen to the wind, he discovered that it still sang to him, still found a way to coax the melodies out of the frost-dusted needles which coated the sentinel trees...albeit softly, very softly indeed.

Patting down his oily long locks over his scalp with a wool-gloved hand, so that small traces of the grey knitted fibers clung to the plastered-down hair after he placed his hand on one hip, Alredge Merewode briefly checked the position of the descending sun in the already darkening sky, deciding that he could still circle the lake once or possibly twice before it became too dark for him to walk back to the University in time for the last tea of the day.

But he only managed to propel himself forward by ten feet or so before he stopped, brow furrowed with unvoiced concern, and stood once more upon the ice, listening.

This time, he had stopped before the reedy accompaniment to his skate-song could cease its repeat of his performance, so he found himself cocking an ear toward the spot he had so recently quitted, the southerly tangle of ice-trapped bent and upright dead reeds.

Despite the quick beat of silence which followed his sudden halt on the ice, Merewode felt it deep in his bones—this was the spot which sang a wordless duet in keeping with each push and glide of his skate blades. This spot...and no other.

"No sense...it makes no sense," the cleric mouthed softly; the loch was ringed with intermittent bunches of the dead vegetation, around its entire circumference. Yet, the sound (cut short a moment too late for its own good) had seemed so definite in its direction, so *specific*—

Softly chanting "No sense, no sense," in time with each push forward on the ice, Alredge narrowed his eyes, to better focus on the sounds rather than the sights around him, as he deliberately altered the pacing of his skate-strokes on the ice, left foot long, right foot short, left short, right long, then long, long, short, long...but whether or not it made any sense, the low hooting whistle of the wind kept perfect time with his erratic ice-rhythm.

And it grew ever so slightly louder with each southward pass around the small oval loch....

Momentarily closing his eyes, Merewode let the wind's malleable fingers caress his cheeks, his forehead, his pursed lips, while he concentrated on the unknown partner in this icy duet; the sound was not unlike a reed flute, or a recorder, yet less defined, almost like a breath-driven percussion instrument with no definite notes or scale *per se*, and no specific pitch. Rather like blowing across the *moue*-tight mouth of a bottle—

His field of vision, deeply red-hazed through his closed eyelids, the Reverend soon found himself losing his physical bearings, and it was only the touch of the frost-kissed reeds against his hands and thighs that warned him that he was skating too close to the thin dark ice near the partially submerged reeds. Opening his eyes to a blinding patch of whiteness, Merewode managed to push himself backwards on the ice, away from the danger of the brittle patch before him. And when he blinked, he saw blooming transparent afterimages, silent fireworks of flickering green and red, which cleared away far slower than real fireworks might have dissolved from his sight.

Only when his vision was true did he look downward, toward the reed-embedded ice which hugged the shoreline...but what he saw (thought he saw) beneath a translucent patch in the center of the sharp-angled dead reeds gave him pause, to the point of making him place a protective gloved hand over his still-opened eyes, while he silently told himself, *It was a fish, it was a beastie, it was nothing.... I didn't see it move, I didn't—*

It was then that the unknown partner in his frigid duet made an almost tentative *swoosh?* of a keening hooting noise, a lonely, yet somehow persistent sound, one which was independent of the breeze which teased and caressed Merewode's exposed cheeks and forehead, and played *I've-got-it* with his cold-tipped nose. And, reacting with an almost primitive urge he later regretted, Alredge Merewode removed the shielding hand from his eyes, and stared into the ice-windowed depths of the loch, down at the spot where, what he didn't see move before, most definitely moved again.

White-against-white flesh moved under the previously still dark waters, causing small irregular bubbles to cluster around the pursed lips, and the submerged reed-ends, as the noise began again, still echoing the sound and meter of Alredge's blade-strokes. And as the water-distorted lips and cheeks alternatively puckered and distended, other submerged bits of vegetation undulated in time with that watery woodwind solo, even as the long hair surrounding the head slowly, dreamily, waved and billowed in place.

Even the open eyes were white....

"Statue," he whispered. "Something the pagans cast off when they learned of the word of God...something made by man, to be falsely worshiped by him," even as the cleric knew in his man's heart (which he'd had long before he'd given over his surrounding body to the Lord) that no statue could blow bubbles beneath the icy water...especially not when the surrounding water was relatively calm. But the figure still moved, as if surrounded by wind and not a gelid blanketing of slushy water, and it still stared (as if indeed its white eyes contained an equally white pupil) up at Alredge, while the reed-encircling lips continued their skate-metered movements, despite the lack of accompaniment from him.

"Music-box figurine," he half-reasoned, remembering the fantastic mechanical beings he'd seen on holiday in the Rhine, even as he plainly saw that the movements below him were too elastic, too supple for a construct of metal and *papier-mâché*... and it continued to blow bubbles, hinting of more than a mere bellows within the white-draped chest.

"Trick of the light, trick of the sun on ice," he implored, his voice all but overshadowed by the *fortissimo* swell of the breath-amplified reeds, as the hand of the white form below him rose up above its head, and the pale fingers worked the reeds, as the melody suddenly became complex, and he could almost swear he heard elements of the musical scale—

"Gasses rising from a dead maiden," he verbally decided, even as her eyelids fluttered, and even as her lips released the reeds, before forming silent words. "She has been killed, and thrown in the waters of Loch Coventina...the water has bleached her, the waters now animate her limp flesh." Merewode's voice was more brittle than thin ice, and equally pale in tone as he hurried away from the patch of dead, bent reeds, toward the northeast, where the University with its warm rooms, flickering gas lights and steaming pots of tea awaited him, his skate blades snick-*snick*ing in short, *staccato* swipes on the sun-glared ice, and his arms pumping in time with the muffled thuds of his man's heart...until the plaintive sound of the breath-blown reeds behind him cut through the icy snick of his blades, and the whistling hoot of his own tortured breath.

A maiden, true...but perhaps *not* yet dead. Cold unto death, cold past active struggle for release from the icy embrace of the sluggish waters, but perhaps not yet dead-cold—

Turning so quickly on the loch that his blades sent up a feathery spume of shaved ice in his wake, Alredge raced back to the tangle of brush and reeds, and peered down, his face far closer to the ice than before, at the figure beneath the waters and film of protective ice. White was her hair, yet young was her face, and beneath the adhering drape her bosom was small but upright over her rib cage, and when he moved still closer, he saw the almost classical smooth outlines of her legs and nether regions beneath the clinging garment she wore, and he chided himself, *A statue*...like any in the Royal Museum...any dug up from ruins in Greece or Rome. Women are not shaped and colored and contoured thus...alas. This...image never drew breath, or saw the glare of the sun, or felt air on its flesh. Only a trick of the waters, only a cunning contrivance of the sun's dying rays.

Yet, as if in counterpoint to each scolding thought, each mental rebuke, the white woman continued to blow the ends of the reeds, continued to gracefully finger the notes along the length of each submerged reed, and the sounds she produced were sweet beyond hearing, like, yet unlike, hymns of praise, for this was a melody far, far older than any hymn which rose up to a specific God, a melody far more free and unfettered than any designed to show respectful praise and thankfulness to the All Mighty.

And, as he stared with eyes grown watery from the slanting last rays of the western sun, between the notes she used one hand, then the other, to beckon him, a motion unmistakable in its playfulness and lack of dire urgency.

The white woman needed no saving, of the physical or spiritual variety—of *that*, the good cleric was certain beyond a need for any words to that effect.

"Water demon," he spat out through numb rough lips, even as his eye lingered on the ever-less-distinct round smoothness of her plump limbs and her swelling bosom. "Pagan devil...seek your worshipers elsewhere," he added, through lips which trembled from cold rage, then pivoted in place before gliding off for the distant University; but with the coming of evening came the cessation of the breeze, so that the sound of her bubbling melody (which slowly, purposefully, once again became a reed/skate duet on thin ice) grew all the louder and distinct to Alredge's cold-tingling ears.

And with each note of her *obbligato* came the mental accusations: You could save her. Save her soul. If she lives, there's a soul. The pagans were reformed. The pagans adapted. Pagans believed. Their idols could too. Save her. Save her soul.

(Save her body—)

Save her. Redeem her. Purify her. She can hear you. She'll listen. Talk to her.

(Come to her—)

Say the Words. Sing the hymns. Save her.

The descending sun cast a sheen of silky gold across the ice, and its dull radiance half-blinded Alredge as he raced back to the brushy tangle, and the cold window within it; the surrounding trees cast gnarled fingers of shadow across the ice, but enough light filtered down through them to touch her sunken flesh, and impart a false glow of living warmth there. And while her eyes were all white, they could see; when he peered over at her, she stopped breathing into the reeds, and instead pursed her lips, forming a solo kiss in his direction.

The cleric's lips began to form a puckered reply when he noticed how the sun brought out the *bas-relief*-like texture of her cheeks, and the unmistakable pattern of white-on-white scales there—

"No animal, no beast, has a true soul!" The words jittered and skittered on his trembling lips and tongue, tumbling into the air like jagged chunks of ice falling from a warm roof. Yet she still kept her lips pursed, as if waiting for the touch of his lips upon hers, even as he stiffly turned and began to skate away from her across the oft-scored surface of the ice; with each frantic swipe and release of the blades, the furrows in the ice grew deeper, and began to spread in jagged forks like earth-trapped lightning, across the surface of the loch's south end.

And as the sun vanished behind the pointed spires of the surrounding trees, leaving the loch draped in cold darkness, the brittle white skin of Loch Coventina parted just long enough to swallow the forward-moving figure on its surface, with a *staccato* smack and sucking gulp, before the fresh wound in the lake's surface began to smooth over once more with a scab of thinnest black ice, so thin that the darting movements of the man and the woman below the freshly-formed surface might have been easily discerned, had there been people there to witness their silent duet in the cold, cold dark waters.

AFTERWORD

In 1992, Workman Publishing put out a seventeenth-anniversary edition of their 1975 B. Kliban cartoon collection, *Cat*, which included sixteen pages of color drawings in the middle of the book. If you can find that small paperback, there's an atmospheric study of a sweater-wearing cat ice-skating toward a distant yellow rectangle of light amidst the twilight-hued surrounding landscape featured on both the back of the book, and the ninth color print within the book. *That* inspired *this* story, strange as it may seem. Naturally, I couldn't very well write about an ice-skating cat, so I came up with this...and the concept of a submerged statue was something else which had been lingering in the back of my mind, so I finally was able to utilize that.

Ironically, I've never ice-skated in my life (my balance is too poor), so I ended up having my poor "hero" skate far too close to the edge, so close that under normal circumstances he would've crashed through the ice long before he actually did. My bad....

INITIAL APPEAL

May 6. Three more whiskers. On my chin this time, the tweezers didn't meet closely enough to pull them out completely on the first try, so I ended up spending a quarter of an hour bending over the bathroom sink down the hall—and hoping the other tenants wouldn't come knocking at the door—trying to pluck out the miserable stubby things. Have to remember to pick up a new pair next time I'm in the drug store, also tampons.

Got my proof sheets for "The Mouth That Wouldn't Die" from *B.Q.*, as usual with a note asking me to "get these back asap, running late," etc. Only three typos, all minor. Another thing, pick up cotton balls at the d.s., too.

May 8. Think I jinxed myself, buying new tweezers. *Five* whiskers, three on my upper lip (*gross*), the others per usual on the chin. Looks like more might be coming; there's a dark peppery coloration under my skin. I feel like Dustin Hoffman in *Tootsie*, only he *was* a guy. Maybe waxing would do it, but *damn* it hurts.

Editor from *Bloodbath Quarterly* called: would I consider some last minute fine-tuning on the "Mouth..." tale, nothing major, just a few lines at the end? I dictated new lines over the phone, sure glad no one but the dogs were around. I could *feel* two more whiskers pop out. This keeps up, I'll be mistaken for Wolfie or Duke by the landlord. The boys looked up at me with those tongue-lolling sloppy pink doggie grins, but I wasn't in the mood to join them in their mirth.

May 11. I think I will get—no matter the expense—a computer, a word processor, and especially one of those dinguses that hooks one computer to another by phone. *Any*thing so that I don't have to face anyone at that Post Office again. Jeeze, I mean the goon behind the counter didn't *have* to be so *ob*vious, so god-damned *pointed* about staring at my upper lip and chin, as if it were a sign of mental instability and gross metabolic abnormality to have a little bit (*ok,* a lot) of fuzz growing there. I'm surprised that he didn't ask me if I was on the Pill (I'm not, but maybe I'll have to tell people that I am if they get curious—oh-mi-*gawd*, don't let it get that bad!) or, a bit more on the tacky side, ask me if I belonged to a Mediterranean race. And me with light brown hair. If this crap keeps up, I won't be able to go out, period. I'm getting so bad that I'm starting to take a second look at those *glitchy* "Remove Unwanted Hair Forever!" ads in the backs of my women's mags.

Not that it is *that* bad.

May 13. Received my first check for "The Mouth That Wouldn't Die"; wonder if I can get direct deposit service at the bank, the kind senior citizens use. There is the automatic teller, but I hate messing with a machine, and besides, one of my neighbors down the hall got ripped off when she put a check endorsed for deposit only in one of those overnight boxes, and instead of crediting her checking account, some sticky-fingers employee at the bank cashed it or deposited it or *something* and took the money, and *she* had to make good on all the checks she inadvertently bounced.

Maybe my old bottle of Neet would work. I don't think a hat with a veil would go with my jogging suit, or with the over-size tees.

Thank goodness I *can* get food delivered to my apartment. As for the dogs, they can do their duty on newspapers.

May 16. I don't think that this is just "a little mustache problem," as Jessica Lang's character told Hoffman's Dorothy Michaels in

Tootsie. And it may just be that I'm not eating right—who *can* afford to do that on freelance wages?—but...*shit*, I'm not losing weight anywhere *else*, so why up there? Getting dressed this morning, I looked like a little girl who's trying on her mother's flopper-stopper, only there's no flop to stop....At this rate, I'll need to pad the cups out with rolled up socks, only I don't go out except to the bathroom, so why bother? Still, I hate to bounce, for however long I *will* be bouncing.

May 17. Editor at *B.Q.* sent me a photo of the cover of the latest issue, b/w, but I can still see that it's going to be a stunner. I've had my name on the covers of quite a few zines, but this is the first time a cover illo has been based on *my* story. I like the way the artist put the reflection of the killer on the old man's teeth, inside that drooling, gasping mouth. And next to that: "A Hair-"Raising Tale of Neighborly Revenge 'The Mouth That Would Not Die,' by D. B. Winston." (I liked the slight title change; a bit more important-sounding, almost Lovecraftian.) If only Grampa Winston could have seen this! But, if he could see the cover, he'd be able to see *me*.

I wonder if that old wives' tale about shaving making hair grow thicker is true.

May 20. Had to laugh at myself this morning. Not that it's *funny,* but...but sometimes you have to laugh, or else. Picture it: me, in my housecoat and floating bra (empty cups hovering in front of my snap-like nipples), leaning across the communal sink next to the bathroom mirror, taking peeks over my shoulder for the other tenants, wielding my Lady (!) Bic across my bristled, lathered face, noting for the first time that I have a feathering of curled hairs across my chest, just under the Adam's apple....I looked like a fraternity pledge during Rush Week; the campus he-man hunk dolled up for initiation night.

Just remembered something. I haven't had to trim my hair since my last cut. In February. It hasn't even begun to curl down below my ears.

May 24. My contributor's copies arrived; the ed. put a little note in with them, letting me know that in this year's *Bloodbath Reader Survey* I was the fifth most requested author, etc. There was more, but I wasn't in a mood to keep reading. I mean, he doesn't *know*. The guy's had more practice shaving than I have. The little scrap of toilet paper I put on my cut keeps falling off. Didn't Dad use something called a styptic pencil?

The dogs can't seem to quit *smelling* me; they seem puzzled. Last time they acted this way was when my old neighbor Fred Ferger came to visit, back in Wisconsin. They were all over old Fred. God, I hope I'm not smelling like an old *man*!

May 30. I think that my voice is changing. When I answered the phone this morning, the *B.Q.* editor asked if I was home. I don't know if he bought my line about a bad connection, but I kept crinkling a piece of paper next to the receiver, so I think maybe it worked. The call was about that novella I sent in—did I mind if he split it into three sections? I almost suggested that he print it a sentence at a time until kingdom come, but why should I take this mess out on him like that?

Could this be hormones acting up? I'm tempted to write in to one of those newspaper docs, and hope that he prints my letter, but I can just see the reply: "Get thee to a doctory, young... woman(?)." Damn, now I'm fracturing Shakespeare. As if it were *his* fault, too.

Wolfie and Duke are looking at me funny. They growl when I scratch their ears.

June 4. It is more than hormones.

Oh yes. Much more than that.

A long time ago, Grampa Winston told me about this girl who lived in the eighteenth or nineteenth century, who was riding a horse, or maybe running or *some* strenuous thing, and she leaped across a fence or something or other, and even though she was a girl going up and over, she came down a boy...as in she was really male all along, only she hadn't *descended*. Down there. (Grampa said "The fruit was hidden in the tree.") It must have been a bitch for the girl, in those sexually dark times, but maybe she hadn't begun to sprout hair, or didn't have a pair of boobs to lose....I suppose I was lucky to have some warning, before....

For what *that's* worth. But DAMMIT, I wasn't leaping over a fence, I was only bending over to put the dog's dishes on the *floor*. For a moment I thought that it was my period, but something didn't feel *right*....It was like I'd done a number in my pants, but in the *front*. Oh, I don't know how to describe it...a fullness? A presence?

I refuse to go to the bathroom standing up. No *way*!

Before...*this*...I had considered going to a doctor, thought about leaving the apartment, going down to the subway, enduring the stares from supposedly jaded NYC dwellers who stare anyhow, going to a strange doctor (how ironic, I'm usually so healthy that I hadn't needed to get a doctor since moving here), then... showing, and explaining...and, the hell with that, *now*. If I went out today, and wore my jogging pants, running shoes and loose top, no one would take a second look at me...and no one would believe that I'm a woman, either. I don't want to be helped into one of those one-size-fits-all jackets and carted off to Bellevue.

I snuck down the hall to the bathroom, locked the door. I was naked; I looked in the mirror.

I wasn't *me* anymore. Not on the outside, and hell, what else do people see first but the outside of a person?

When I came back to the apartment, the dogs snarled at me.

June 9. I went out, late last night. The dogs weren't as hard to handle as they used to be; my muscle tone must be better, or the muscles themselves are bigger. My jeans fit, but funny—the rear end is baggy, and they don't hang right. Maybe I could order some men's jeans from a catalog, but that would be giving in to...this. Something I hate to do. Came home, started a story. No one's seen me, I hope. Have to keep making money. Can't risk being thrown out *now*. Maybe I'll submit the story to one of the flesh zines; they pay pretty damn good. I've got a couple of stories out in men's magazines, both under a pseudonym. Clarke Dennis. It would have been my name, if...I had been born the way I am now.

I think that I can get this finished by tomorrow, and send it off...at night.

June 13. Over a month now, since *this* started. Soaping my body in the shower (at midnight, when no one wants in there), I noticed that the skin tone is different; thicker, and even tougher in places. And more hairy, of course. Even my bones seem heavier, behind my ears the cartilage is bigger, and my ears stick out. My nails—all short, for a change—are broader, and slightly ridged. Unfortunately, I'm not taller. My weight has gone up, from 135 (ok—nearly 140) to 155, most of it muscle. Luckily, I have a good supply of elastic waist shorts and men's tees, bought during a white sale back home in Ewerton. I rinse out my things and hang them in my room; I can't face the laundry room downstairs.

Good Lord. I hope my folks don't ever call me.

June 22. I think I know what has happened, what *is* happening to me. On the 10th I sent in "The Metamanphosis" to *Skin Magazine*, and the assistant editor there recognized my name, and forward my story *pronto* to the fiction editor, who had previously bought a story from me. Only instead of writing to let me know he was buying my story (as he had done previously) the man called. And asked for D. B. Winston, the name written in the upper right-hand corner of my ms., only when I answered, he didn't seem surprised that I was a woman, or man, or whatever I happened to sound like. He and I chatted for a few minutes; he let me know how much I'd be getting for the story (more than enough), then, before he hung up, he commented, "You had me going there for a while, D.B.; the parts of the story where the protagonist is still a woman are fantastic—I almost believed that you *are* a woman! God, man, that is no mean feat...

one more thing, do you still want this under the 'Clarke Dennis' name or would you like to have it run under...ok...I'll keep the Dennis byline on it. Well, D. B., thanks for submitting..." etc., and when he finally hung up I began to paw through my files (in the old cardboard box I keep under my bed), looking for all my correspondence, rejection slips, contracts, and the like.

After I found what I wanted, I spread the mass of papers out on the floor (the dogs lay off to the side, heads on paws, rumbling at me), and began scanning them carefully.

It was all there, in unwavering black on white. My name, "D. B. Winston," on my contracts, no "Debbie," no "Ms.," or "Miss," or any indication that "D. B. Winston" was a woman. Likewise, those zines who either sent handwritten rejection slips, or personalized the form ones were all similar—either "Dear D. B.," "Dear D. B. W.," or "Dear D. B. Winston," or, worse, "Dear Mr. Winston"...something which hadn't bothered me before. When I was still outwardly a woman. Then, the loss of my feminine identity wasn't a pressing concern...why should it have been? *I* knew who I was, *what* I was...what did it matter that other people weren't in the clear about it?

At the time, it didn't seem *important*, it actually didn't *matter*.

I picked up one of the rejection slips, from a small press zine, with my now blunt and stubby-fingered hand. The editor had typed, "All this time, my husband and I thought D. B. Winston was a man! What a surprise to see you sign your name 'Ms.'" That letter, the cover letter to a story I sent to her, was a rarity on my part, and I never signed another one that way....A few years ago, I once sent a fan letter to Robert Bloch, and even *he* addressed his postcard reply to "Mr. D. B. Winston"...and to think that it seemed *humorous* at the time. With a growing certainty, I scanned the contributor's copies of the many zines which ran my material, and was confronted with page after page of fiction credited only to "D. B. Winston" (and noticed all that junk mail in my wastebasket addressed to "*Mr.* D. B. Winston"; why even the computer mailing lists had an erroneous view of my gender!), and on top of it, zines like *Bloodbath Quarterly* and

Skin didn't run author's pages (even if they did, people seldom read them)...and many of the stories I'd written were told from a *man's* point of view. Right from the start, most of the writers in the horror genre were *men*...which was the main reason I'd used my initials only on submitted material. I'd read once in an article about breaking into the writing field that men have the edge when it comes to selling certain types of fiction, and since I wasn't fond of my name in the *first* place (to me, Deborah Bambi Winston always sounded so cotton-candy-cheerleader-from-Queen-Disneyland-sorority-sister-*cutesy*, and plain old Debbie Winston had a small-town-lumber-mill-office-clerk feel to it), using my initials seemed so appealing, so natural, so crisply efficient...and, unbeknownst to me, so *masculine*.

Crazy as that sounds, it does make sense; wasn't that editor surprised to find out that I was a woman, which in turn meant that the impression she'd gotten that I was a man was a strong one? After all, didn't Peter Pan, or one of those fairy tale kiddies, say that "wishing makes it so?" If that's the case, wouldn't "thinking makes it so" also apply? I remembered the *B.Q.* editor's note, the one he included with my contributor's copies...the one with the readers' survey results. That meant a lot of readers who looked for my stories, and if I had had my doubts before—Winston was a man. I got out the letter, and if I had had my doubts before—

"...fifth most requested author, behind Bloch and Williamson and Koontz, and you'd be surprised which authors you topped. Funny, some of the readers added comments in the margins about their favorites, and about you they wrote, "he's my favorite," and "That Winston dude scares me!" I guess the readers really got into those macho-hero adventures about pagan sacrifices and bird-blood worship you wrote while you were still living in...."

—*that* was the capper. Odd, even though I now know (*think* I know) what happened, I'm no better off than before...like, I can't do any—

Thought of something. More later.

July 2. My hands and fingers aches, my eyes are blurred from staring at endless black letters marching across illuminated white paper, my tongue is coated with that awful gummy taste from licking too many stamps and envelope flaps...but I think this may work. Might work. Has *got* to work. Pleaseplease*please* work.

In less than two weeks I have written eight short stories, three poems, and a criticism of faceless-personality-less-mind-less killers in 1980s teen slasher flicks. Plus cover letters for each submission with my full name, *Deborah Bambi Winston*, as in "Miss" and "Ms." etc. on each one, and on the upper-right hand corner of each first page. And all the rest of the pages, for good measure. I'll mail them all, twelve different envelopes for as many different zines (all the ones I submit to who don't know I'm a female...*inside*), but I'll wait until darkfall to leave the apartment.

July 25. Maybe it will work. My chest feels plump in places, the *right* places. And *it* seems shorter, not that I examined it much to begin with. Keep thinking *girl*, *girl*, I am a *girl*, chant it like a litany....

Aug. 1. The hair on my chest is thinning, fine and almost gone from under the now slight protuberance on my throat. Got back two ms., with slips attached for a *"Miss* Winston." Much better. One poem sold; the check is made out to "Ms. Deborah B. Winston"—I guess the "Bambi" part was a bit much for the poor editor! Got a packet of fan mail (!) from *B.Q.*, a few were addressed to "Mr. or Ms. Winston," and one was for a "Miss"! Also, a b/w mock-up of the next cover, with the *full* name, etc.

The dogs are licking my hands and letting me pet them again.

Aug. 16. I'm almost big enough upstairs to *wiggle* when I walk! A bit disconcerting with the remainder of the chest hair, but I'll live! Two rejection slips, made out for "Ms. Winston." One sale, no check yet. The editor from *B.Q.* called, said my phone line sounded clearer. Part one of the "Deborah Bambi Winston" novella will be out September 2. I may be able to throw out the tweezers and shave cream yet!

Aug. 30. Plucked out what I pray is the last whisker this morning. Can show my face in the hallway again, neighbors claimed they missed me. Weight down to 141. *That* is gone now, almost, retracting from whence it came, for eternity, I hope. (Never *did* give in and urinate standing up.) Today I will go shopping out in the mid-day sun, and never mind the ultraviolet rays. Cancer can't be much worse than...what *happened.*

Sept. 4. Got the check for "The Metamanphosis" from *Skin.* I'd almost forgotten that I'd sold that one...*wanted to forget*, actually. I'll have to contact the editor and have him change the byline. He'll probably get a kick out of the "Bambi" part. I'll write him a note after stopping at the bank, and walking the boys.

Sept. 5. It's out. In the stores. *Skin Magazine*, with the "Clarke Dennis" byline and story title on the front cover. My contrib. copies came late, bulk rate, sent in late August. The editor put in a note. Said how much he loved the story. Said the first part *almost* fooled him. Said he enjoyed talking with me in July. Said I should subscribe, cut-rate to his zine, that I'd like it. Said his readers were bound to go nuts over the story. Said I seem like a really great guy.

He's right. Sort of.

I am a great guy.

In a few places here and there this time.

AFTERWORD

Those readers who have already bought my other Borgo collection *Ewerton Death Trip*, or who may have seen the classic

1980s digest-sized horror magazine *Night Cry* are probably familiar with my story "Dear D. B. ..."; it was in the final issue of *N.C.*, and was also a fairly popular download on the now defunct Alexandria Digital Literature site. But *this* version is the fate I originally intended for Deborah Bambi Winston— however, the editor at *N.C.* thought it was too literal to qualify as a *N.C.* story, so he suggested that I try rewriting it, which I did. I do agree that this is a tad literal, but, then again, so was Gregor Sama's transformation in *The Metamorphosis*. (*Not* that my story is in the same league as Kafka's masterpiece!)

As rough-edged as this is, I still like it, and have been trying for years without success to interest editors into running it (even for free) as a specialty item, to no avail—but, given the fact that I have other multiple-version variants of a couple of other stories out there, in various magazines and collections, I thought this one deserved to be published, too.

Personally, I find both versions of the story somewhat flawed; this one for obvious reasons, but I'm not 100% fond of "Dear D. B. ..." simply because I didn't have the opportunity to do a much-needed revamp/rewrite on it prior to it getting published—*N.C.*'s editor knew that the magazine was folding soon, and wanted one last story from me in it...and "Dear D. B. ..." was in his submission pile, so he ran with it as-is. One comment I received from Peggy Nadramia over at *Grue* was especially apt—she noted that D. B. would have to have a slew of odd jobs on the side in order to survive in New York City, even living in a low-rent hovel. That is something I would have liked to have addressed in the story, but I'm not planning on rewriting something which is already fairly well-known. But Peggy's point was well taken....

The incident which actually inspired me to write this one was the misidentification of me as a male writer in an early small press appearance—at the time I thought it was funny, and only gradually considered the notion of public perception influencing bodily reality....

MOTHER GOTHEL
AND PERSINETTE

Of all the flowering trees in her garden, the sorceress Mother Gothel loved her persimmon tree the best; a wandering witch from the distant island called Kyushu presented it to Mother Gothel as a token of her affection, and each summer, when the red-orange berries ripened, their sweet ovals, when sliced in half before the succulent tasting, reminded Mother Gothel of that witch's hidden, deep pink sweetness.

Thus, whenever Mother Gothel tended to her garden, she spent the most time near that special tree, counting each ripening fruit, and savoring each minute spent in anticipation of her harvest-time feast...and its accompanying memories, for in the land where she dwelled other sorceresses and witches were scarce indeed, and often the years were long and lonely between her all-too-brief times of shared passion. Mother Gothel's only neighbors were a married couple who lived on the other side of the high stone wall which surrounded her garden, and their mutual happiness was too complete to allow the wife to offer any such joy to Mother Gothel...but when the sorceress entered her private garden one afternoon, she discovered the husband plucking the smooth-fleshed ripe persimmons from the lower branches of her love-token tree, his vest pockets already stuffed with the sweet berries, even as his hands held still more berries.

"How dare you sneak into my garden and steal what is rightfully mine? Did *you* grow this fruit, that you feel obligated to fest upon it?" she hissed through her snaggle teeth, as the frightened neighbor man stammered, "N-not for me...it is my wife who craves these sweet berries. Without them, she would die of hunger, and starve the child growing within her—"

The mention of a child piqued the interest of Mother Gothel, for in her case, the appellation "Mother" was a term of respect among her fellow magic-makers and spell-casters, not an indication of her own fruitfulness. And since she was a woman wise in the ways of divination, she looked up at the window in the neighbor's house, the high one which overlooked her garden, and by making some signs with her gnarled fingers, and peering through the configuration of her overlapping hands, it became known to her that the child growing within the belly of the neighbor-woman was a girl...a girl-child who would become a woman, with the secret sweetness only a woman possesses.

Deciding that the stolen berries might be worth that future— the sorceress uncrossed her hands, and said as she stared at the frightened neighbor through her cloudy blue eyes, "Keep the fruit you have taken...but in payment, I want the fruit of your wife's labors in return. Take as many more of my berries as she needs, as long as I am given the child—" (Mother Gothel didn't let on that she knew the child *would* be a girl) "—once it has been born. And fear not, the child will thrive as my garden thrives."

Seeing the sorceress' garden *was* a lush paradise of tall-growing trees and many-petaled flowers, the husband agreed to Mother Gothel's request.

That harvesting time, Mother Gothel only savored but a few fragrant red-gold berries, but come early winter, she was given a gift of a girl-child, carried into her garden by the neighbor couple, who were grateful that they'd escaped the wrath of their conjuring neighbor, and be allowed to live out their lives unscathed (which is what the couple did do; and they had many more children, none of whom were nourished on a diet of persimmon berries while waiting to be born), simply by giving up the milk-skinned baby with the flaming orange-red thatch of wavy hair, which did not match that of either parent, but instead came from the colorful sweet fruit her mother had consumed.

Once the couple had tip-toed out of Mother Gothel's enchanted flowering garden, the sorceress raised the autumn-haired girl-child as tenderly and as attentively as her beloved persimmon tree; as a sign of her interest in the child, Mother Gothel named her Persinette, both for her flaming hair and for her pre-birth diet.

But Mother Gothel thought not of the child as a daughter, for even though she was an enchantress, she was also once a human being, with the same needs and aches and longing of a woman...but, even as she was well-versed in the black arts, and the ways of magic and spell-casting, she was also moral, in her own dark way, and thus she envisioned the fire-haired girl not as her daughter, but as her *some*-day love; but, just as the berries of her dearly-thought-of Asian witch-woman's gift-tree were not fit for the tasting until they were fully ripe, so was Persinette not suitable for the taking by Mother Gothel, even as she longed to partake of the girl's hidden sweetness.

So, as the girl grew closer to her sixteenth winter, and her time of ripeness, and the temptation all but overcame Mother Gothel, she cast a spell over the stones and the mud, in the field near her humble sorceress' abode, and caused to be built a tall, tall, tower, with but a single room at the top. And it was in this room that she placed Persinette, who by this time had hair longer than the number of hours in a day, glorious, rippling bright hair caught up in two rope-thin braids which the young woman wore in a crown-like coil atop her head. Whenever Mother Gothel's desire to feast her cloudy eyes upon the young lady grew too overpowering (just as she often sat under her beloved persimmon tree, and gazed at the slowly ripening fruit amid the dark oblong leaves), Mother Gothel would stand at the base of the tower and implore:

> *"Persinette, beloved Persinette,*
> *Uncoil your hair for me."*

And down would flow the silken braids, upon which the sorceress would climb to the top of the tower (even though she possessed the ability to fly to the top), until she be so tired upon her arrival that she could literally do no more than feast her eyes upon the budding beauty of Persinette, and watch the continual growth and maturation of her gift-child into a fruitful ripe woman, even as her mouth watered in anticipation....

But it so happened one day, that when she finished her climb to the top of the tall, tall tower, then sat exhausted upon Persinette's narrow maiden's bed, she noticed a gently-rounded swelling beneath the flowing gown of the henna-haired girl, right above the hidden sweetness within her. Noticing Mother Gothel's pointed stare, the girl asked sweetly, "Mother Gothel, why are my clothes becoming tight?"

And despite her already certain intuition about the origin of that swelling beneath Persinette's simple gown, Mother Gothel made the secret configurations with her hands, and, when she peered through the open spaces of her fingers, she saw what was resting within the belly of Persinette. Two babies, a boy and a girl...neither of which had been nourished to sweetness on a diet of persimmons.

Keeping the worst of her rage to herself, Mother Gothel stroked that rounded protrusion through Persinette's thin gown, and asked with a sweetness to match that of the girl, "Did something go in you, to leave behind this growing belly?"

Her trust in Mother Gothel still intact, the girl answered dutifully, "A man slept with me, in yonder bed...but he spoke the same words you do, so I knew it was all right to let down my coils of hair for him. He is a man most fine, with most...unusual sources of pleasure—"

Now while Mother Gothel was well-versed in the ways of love of her own kind, she did not take kindly to the thought of a man having his way with her Persinette, especially before she herself had partaken of her love-gift, so, in a rage which caused the errant young woman to stand, shocked into mute silence, in place before Mother Gothel, the sorceress snatched up a sharp bread knife in one hand, and, after she'd grasped Persinette's braids in the other hand, then wound them into a coil upon her fingers, she sawed through the fiery hair, until only a short mane of it covered Persinette's head. But, when the greater length of her tresses were freed, the hair that remained curled and clung so cunningly and so tightly to Persinette's head that the lonely enchantress was captivated by its resemblance to that hair which sheltered the sweet fruit below the girl's now-full belly, and instantly felt her angry heart soften with love and pity for the sadly-used girl.

Using her magic powers, she sent the girl wafting downward on the wind, to her secret, fecund garden, and bade her to dwell in the little well house amid the flowering trees and bushes. Then, in order to quell her desire to savor the already-tasted girl, just in case her condition *was* a sign of full ripeness after all, Mother Gothel busied herself with unraveling the shorn braids, and wound each strand in turn on bobbins she'd carved herself from the fallen branches of her departed witch-woman's persimmon tree. And as she worked, Mother Gothel thought to herself, Each hair is so strong, so supple...much like the string which stretches the simple length of wood into a deadly bow....

And so, knowing as she did the ways of men, especially men most fine bearing sources of unknown (to her, at least!) pleasure, Mother Gothel was well-armed when she heard that harsh (again, to her ears) voice implore:

"*Persinette, Persinette my own,*
Uncoil your wreath of curls."

Peering out from the lone window of the tall tower room, she saw the man standing far below her, looking up toward the distant window—and, perhaps because the window *was* so far away, he did not realize that the finger-thin arrow which was aimed at his heart was, indeed, an arrow (and not the tip of one of Persinette's braids) until it had been propelled by Persinette's springy-hair-bow, and it sank deep into his manly, fine chest....

* * * * * * *

And once Persinette's belly-ripened to the point of full persimmon-berry-like roundness, Mother Gothel was there to deliver her twins, which—once they were wrapped in downy blankets, and tucked into a wooden box fashioned of cured persimmon wood slats—were dutifully left under the cover of darkness at the door of the neighbor couple, who always seemed to have room to spare for yet another child.

And, because Mother Gothel was so good to Persinette in her time of confusion (the pain of the birth alone was enough to convince the young woman that unusual sources of pleasure had most unpleasant consequences), once the secret places within her had healed, and longed once more for pleasure, Persinette gladly let Mother Gothel partake of her sweetness and ripened juices, for now she was truly a woman fit for the tasting, which Mother Gothel did most gladly and gratefully.

And so it came to pass that the two women shared the task of caring for the aged persimmon tree which had brought both of them such gladness, and such fruitful times of pleasure and because the blood and bones and flesh of the fine young man nourished the persimmon tree so well, it too enjoyed its most fruitful time of life, giving forth sweet berries which bore a glistening red-orange hue, each of which was savored by Mother Gothel and her sweet love Persinette.

AFTERWORD

This story originally appeared under one of my erotica pen names, mainly because at the time I felt it was a little too out there for my main audience. Looking it over now, I think it is a slightly better fit for this collection than for any of my purely erotica e-books over at Circlet Press.

I came up with this after reading through a volume of uned-ited/non-bowdlerized *Grimm's Fairy Tales*, which included an appendix of supplementary material in the back—in it, I learned that an early version of the *Rapunzel* story had different character names, which I used here. In many ways, I'm not totally sure *why* I wrote this; I suppose I was trying to approach fairy tales form a different point of view. I think it may have been written for one of those slightly-more-adult fairy tale anthos which were published back in the 1990s, but I cannot remember for sure now. At any rate, it wasn't accepted if I did write it for that antho....

I suppose being sexually abused by my grandmother may have had something to do with this; I'm not 100% crazy about this story, but it's here, and I figured someone might like it, or at any rate might find it of some interest....

LITTLE NIPS

"I wish I had a buck for every time someone has asked me that same question." She took another drag on her half-spent cigarette, holding the smoke in as if it were a joint instead of a hard-pack menthol, then letting it out through her nose where tiny wisps of steam-fine smoke filtered out from the piercings above each nostril even as the rest of the smoke billowed out from the pair of there-from-birth nostril-holes—and she smiled again when she noticed my slightly appalled stare. When she smiled, the ball-tipped studs in her lower lip, tongue-tip and upper lip winked in the bar's neon beer-sign lights like miniature Christmas tree bulbs strung across the bottom of her face; tiny winking orbs of flashing green, blue and red, joined by thread-fine chains of silver rather than the usual plastic wrapped green wire.

Even after she became silent, waiting for my lame comeback, probably, I could still *hear* her, with each breath, each drag on her smoke, her face (hell, her whole body—or at least what was exposed in that smoke-filled, noisy bar on that smotheringly hot August evening) tinkled softly...a metal-touching-metal chiming/clanging sound that should've been swallowed up in the jabber of voices and discordant layers of drinking and eating noise...but *wasn't*.

The reflective web of chains that looped around and over and into places which were most likely pierced but hidden by her halter and shorts may've been eye-grabbing, but the thing about her which had caught my attention a few minutes earlier was just *how* those loops of chain-work were attached to her body.

This woman who had sat down next to me at the crowded bar wore studs and bars and rings and sharp-pronged French wires in just about every spare bit of flesh that could be easily pinched up and pierced—plus a few places that defied reason or ease of puncturing with a sterilized needle. Tender, thin, vulnerable places, like the edges of her eyelids, or the flesh between her finger—places she nonetheless *had* pierced and subsequently adorned with hair-fine loops of silvery wire and linking chain-mesh. And at the base of each visible puncture, I saw barely-healed, almost raw pinkish spots where the flesh was poked through and through, then adorned with circles and solid balls of shimmering silver. She wore seven earrings in each ear—four holes in each small lobe and the rest poking through the rounded top part. And each earring was chain-attached to some part of her face so that her pasty-pale cheeks were imprisoned by fine links of forged metal radiating from each ear to her upper and lower lips, her nose, and her eyelids and eyebrows. Plus an open-weave headpiece consisting of even more chains which looped over and around her buzzed-bald head so that the ropes of silver rested in a bed of eighth-inch high dyed-black stubble.

And as I said before, that was just her head...more chains dangled down to her nipples, her wrists and between-the-fingers, and even some from her be-ringed navel to some spots below that just had to be pierced, too—why else would she have other chains descending into the waist band of her cut-offs?

She'd taken another dragon-like puff of her cigarette before I thought of a suitable comeback to her non-answer to my question; rooting around in my jeans pocket with my free hand, I finally found a weathered, chamois-soft George Washington—which I ceremoniously placed on the bar next to her half-empty bottle of beer. That made her smile—and reveal a set of teeth dotted by inset specks of silver. By now, the sight of her drilled and filled front teeth didn't shock me as much as it might've only a couple of minutes before.

Picking up the faded bill with a jingling hand, she snubbed

out her cigarette with the other before saying, "Of course it hurts...but the thing people never bother to ask is how much or just how bad. Or not; hell, some women can birth a baby and walk out of the hospital an hour later. It's all a matter of what a person can stand above and beyond *this*"—she fluttered her hand, letting the rings and chains attached to her finger-bases and wrist-bone flash in the too-bright bar lights—"before you put the first stud or hoop in, you know?"

"I faint when I get a splinter," I tried to joke, but now that she knew my interest in her was at least marginally more serious than most of the people who gawked at her, she wasn't about to let the subject drop. Reaching toward my head with her right hand, she smiled that glittering smile of hers and said as her thumb and forefinger made encircling contacts with my earlobes, "Let's see if that's true," before pinching the dangling nub of flesh between her beige-lacquered long nails.

The pain was short, sharp, but not enough to make me faint... more like a little nip from a small animal that's been frightened.

"See?" she smiled as she withdrew her hand, leaving me to rub my earlobe in annoyed silence (I wasn't about to yelp for her, if that's what she expected). But when I saw the blood-smear on my fingers when I stopped rubbing my ear, I began, "Hey, that's not funny—" until she cut in, "Wasn't meant to be. Just giving you your dollar's worth."

"Too bad I don't have an earring to put in there...feels like you've poked a hole in it," I grumbled before finishing the last of my own beer. While my bottle was still upended, and the slightly warm brew coursed down my throat, she said, "I'll bet it'd look good with a stud. Some gold or maybe silver...if you're brave. Some claim silver's a 'dirty' metal. But since you didn't faint...maybe getting it done wouldn't hurt so much either—"

Wiping the foam off my lips with my free hand, I shook my head *No Way* before saying, "Sorry, I think I'll just go find some peroxide or iodine to clean this...I've *heard* that professional piercers use needles...."

"They do...say, I've got some antiseptic in my car. The least

I can do is clean it up, 'kay? It's on me," she added before getting off her bar stool with a jingle and a metallic whisper of swaying chains, then padding off for the bar's double doors without turning her chains-and-stubble-covered head to see if I was following her. A quick glance at the smoke-grimed bar mirror revealed that I was now sporting a huge, ruddy bead of blood on my earlobe so, after paying for my beer, I hurried after her, all the while assuring myself that I'd only let her sterilize the wound and not shove some hunk of metal through it—even as I patted my condom-carrying pocket in time with each step while picturing all the other places those chains and loops of silver might lead to.

I pretended to believe her claim that she'd forgotten her piercing kit at home; she only lived a short drive away and anyhow, my earlobe had actually stopped hurting so her jibe about "maybe getting it done again" didn't sound so ominous anymore. At least as long as she stayed away from the *really* sensitive parts.

Her place was a walk-up, above a store of some sort. Dark walls, dark furniture, swallow-your-feet-to-the-ankles-thick shag carpeting. Couldn't see too much in the forty-watt bulbs she used in the lamps, but even if they'd been one hundred watts each, I don't think the place would have seemed any brighter...it just smelled dark. Warm-dark, like blood and spices and burnt wood shavings. No radio or stereo played, yet the place was filled with sound; with each step, each movement of her head and arms, I found myself bathed in that metallic tintinnabulation until my brain echoed with the jangle and clinking noises, so much so that I had to strain to hear her instruction for me to sit on the sofa while she got her piercing kit, of her warning that "This'll sting a bit."

I was expecting pain when the peroxide-soaked cotton ball hit my torn lobe, but the sensation was only another tiny nip, followed by a lingering after-burn that wasn't as painful as it was...exhilarating. And the jingling around me seemed so loud I had to shout out, "You're right, it doesn't hurt at all," but she didn't seem to mind the loudness of my voice, for all she did was smile before snapping open the latch on her piercing case and withdrawing something that nipped and stung yet didn't *hurt*-hurt once I closed my eyes and relaxed on that dark upholstered couch, letting her pull up flesh with shivery-cool tugs of her long-handled tongs and give it a little stinging nip before releasing the tongs and moving on to another untouched patch of flesh.

The first thing I was aware of when I awoke was how... complete I now felt; that I was pierced didn't matter because of what was now an extra part of me. Cool metal filled the still-throbbing holes in my flesh, tiny bits and loops and studs which rested against the surrounding nakedness yet somehow took away all previous feeling of vulnerability I'd associated with being bare and exposed. Even the spots which were usually the most sensitive hurt no more than the more typically pierced areas like my earlobes...and while I was no bigger anywhere on my body, the metal adornments made me feel larger, stronger, more *complete* in the fullest sense of the word.

It was only after I'd found and caressed each new metal-plugged hole in my body that I began to remember, in tantalizing, maddeningly incomplete fragments, what she and I had done during and after the piercing...the sight of her pale, chain-crisscrossed nude body with the clanging, tiny loops of silver bisecting her nipples and inner and outer labia; the rough-ribbed sensation of her chains running against my own bare flesh, the individual links and studs grinding into my skin; the little white-hot nip of stimulating pain as she lifted up my penis and pierced the tip with...at that point, my memory was murky-vague, or somehow I didn't have a clear mental picture of her holding anything at all in either hand even as I'd felt that exquisite pinch-and-tear—

Turning over on my side on the well-padded comfortingly-shaggy carpet, I felt her sleeping beside me, her breaths coming up so softly that they were inaudible in the still-dark room, her ornamented flesh pleasantly warm under the cool ropes of confining chains...and when she didn't stir as I slid my hand over and around the small patches of metal-free flesh, I felt confident enough to unclasp one of the chains from the ring adorning her navel, just so I could feel a little more smooth, unencumbered skin—

And even though she began to writhe slightly while I worked to undo more and more of her chains, she said nothing so I felt confident that my actions were pleasing to her; by the time I'd freed her breasts and swollen labia, she began to moan softly, her breaths coming in short, moist hitches, so I quickly began unclasping the silvery bindings which imprisoned her cheeks, her rounded bristle-cover scalp...by that time, her back began to arch upwards as her legs spread slightly, invitingly, so I paused in my labors to begin kissing her unfettered flesh—

—but as my lips touched her skin, it felt almost cold, not warm like I expected it to fell...nor was it as silky-smooth as I remembered it to be. As I pulled my lips from her, I could still taste the surface of her skin—and when I poked my slightly swollen, studded tongue out of my mouth and licked her be-ringed lips, I felt flakes of loose skin which didn't come from my lips—

My fresh piercings ached as I scrambled to my feet and felt my way across one wall, searching for the coffee table and lamp I thought were there; by the time I'd found the table and lamp, I knew I was bleeding in spots, but the pain still felt...good, in a way I now found too hideous to contemplate. And when I clicked on the lamp and yanked off the shade, I forced myself to look at the place where most of her still remained on that long, thickly-napped carpet, even as less and less of her stayed in my line of sight.

Freed of the network of silvery bonds, her flesh wrinkled and pulled in on itself, even as she sank deeper and deeper into the carpeting, until only a soft shadow of pinkish-pale flesh remained, dappled with a peppering of black in a couple of widely-separated spots...no blood, no gurgling rush of decayed flesh, just a wrinkling flattening, *lessening* of her body—save for the silvery studs and circles and fish-hook curving prongs of metal, and those limp chains of silver which rested in ripples and S-curves of unfettered metal links on the thick tufted carpet.

Loose, now useless chains of metal that somehow seemed... *inviting* to my pierced and decorated parts; inside, I was still reeling from what I'd seen, my heart thudding in time with my pounding brain (*Some people claim silver's a 'dirty' metal*), but all those little metal-filled holes in me, all over me, *they* now ached with a different sort of pain. A pain that felt like little nips of *longing*, as if what had felt so complete to me only minutes before was now sadly lacking, sadly useless—

That the chains themselves were free of...her, or lingering traces of her, was somewhat a blessing in itself, but the worst part of that morning was knowing that even if they hadn't been so clean, so pristine, I still would have needed to attach them to my own studs and circles of shining, *dirty* silver.

Not to have done so would've left me feeling so incomprehensibly incomplete, so deeper-than-skin-deep *vulnerable*—

—although lately I wish I had a dollar for every time someone asks me if being pierced again and again like this *hurt*, as if mere pain was the only fear on my mind.

AFTERWORD

Midway through the 1990s, quite a few of the markets where I'd been selling my horror fiction started to shut down or become so overstocked that they were only opening up to submissions every couple of years or so; I'd begun to experiment with harder-core erotic horror and sf, which I soon began selling to markets like Circlet Press. But every so often a story would slide through the cracks—not quite "hot" enough for the erotica publishers, but too erotic for more mainstream genre markets. "Little Nips" was one of these stories...it was also one of my first stories which dealt with body modification, a theme which has popped up in much of my sf from the end of the '00s. It's darker than some of my earlier work, but milder than stories like "Dark Ladonna" or "Yet Another Poisoned Apple for the Fairy Princess." But for what it is, it works, at least for me....

OF VAMPIRES AND GENTLEMEN

Very close to midnight...

...the quiet time when even the gentle inhalation and exhalation of the twenty girls in the dormitory blended in with the nearly soundless flow of night air through sheer white voile-masked windows, the time when the darkness signified not the mere absence of light, but the addition of something missing from the sullen day; an odor that had no definite smell, a pressure in the weightless air, an added heat in a rather cool room—it was then, in that hour that the girls had learned to dub "the vampire time," that Elizabeth abruptly found herself suddenly, totally awake, one hand cradling thinly-covered breast, the other wedged in the place of sparsely hair-covered warmth, pressed hard into the moist nightgown-sheathed hidden spot. And, listening hard, straining her ears in the white noise of muted breathing and endless flowing air, she waited to hear *him*; hear the living flutter of his changeling wings, hear the rustle of his cape as it brushed against the nubby fabric of her coverlet, hear the slight smacking noise his lips would make as they parted, the thin skin of his lips slowly unsealing with an infinitesimal noise, a sound meant for her and her alone. Then, would come the dry rasp as her sheet was lifted from her crisp nightgown, the fragile sound of his dry, cool hand brushing against the lace trim near the buttons on her nightgown...and Elizabeth wondered if buttons made a sound...as they were slipped out of the buttonholes.

That part she hadn't thought of, hadn't imagined, hadn't heard from the other girls. Nor had she told the other girls in her class about that part, during the time she claimed that she, too, had had a "vampire time"...and, luckily, none of the others had thought it an important enough thing to ask about.

Now, as she lay, every inch of her body tensed, warm and ready, waiting for the soft sound of his coming, his time with her, Elizabeth told herself that this time she would really, truly know exactly how everything felt...not that they hadn't believed her before. She had almost believed herself, too, and that was the worst part. Elizabeth didn't want to risk letting the fantasy become too good, too perfect to give up...and it wasn't her fault that the vampire had waited so long to come to her, had waited so long for their time.

Opening her eyes, closing her eyes, it made little difference. Elizabeth settled on eyes half-closed, a sexily dreamy expression that she hoped the vampire would find pleasing. That he must find pleasing. She kept the covers drawn up under her chin like the other girls did. Under the covers, her hands worked silently, slowly, until the moistness spread across the wrinkled folds caught in the twisted hair, and the cloth spread over her chest was taut, flesh working against the tightly woven fabric. Through her slitted eyes, Elizabeth could see the window across the dormitory, the one that faced her bed, and she watched for a darkness to flutter into view behind the filmy curtain. And remembered, as she watched, and waited....

* * * * * * *

Where he had come from, they didn't know. Why he had come to them, they didn't much care. When he had come, they were pretty sure, unless someone had been lucky and kept it a secret before the others 'fessed up.

Cecily had been the first, or the first to tell. They—all the girls in Elizabeth's dormitory, in the freshman class at the Miranda Hawthorne's Young Ladies College, limited enrollment of one hundred girls (no less) per semester, *no* men allowed on campus, weekend passes to upperclassmen only, *no* smoking allowed, *no* liquor, same for drugs, *no* fraternization among the ranks tolerated, *no* pregnancy, *no, no, no* to anything a person had to ask about, a place which turned out Young Ladies of Worth, Well-Educated Ladies; a place where, once their daughters were enrolled (the common term used by Elizabeth's friends was "sentenced") parents would not have to worry about the onrush of Vice and Moonie cultists, where parents could say with pride "My daughter is getting an education" and mean it—were in the long, narrow dormitory bathroom; toweling off, powdering, brushing teeth, flushing, gargling and doing what girls in dormitories all across the country do every morning, talking above the feminine din, when Cecilly's voice cut through the morning noise like a fire siren at a symphony:

"I *was* with a vampire last night!" she said to no one and everyone, as she leaned over one of the mascara-toothpaste-and-soap splotched sinks lining the west wall, touching pink-tipped fingers to her white neck. In seconds she was ringed by nineteen dripping, powdery, half-dressed girls, all trying to press close without touching too much, all straining to see the twin red-lipped holes in her neck. Patty, who was majoring in English Lit and knew about such things as vampires, took over immediately.

Pushing the others aside, she hopped up on the adjoining sink and leaned over, peering at Cecily's neck, asking questions as she looked and gently prodded.

"Do you feel weak?"

"Uh...*sort* of."

"Did you see his shadow on the wall?"

"Was there a full moon? Wait, there was, and he didn't...I mean, no, I didn't see it!"

"Did he walk in or fly away?"

"Both, I mean, he flew in then walked to the window, but I thought it was a dream, see, so I didn't—"

"Did he...uh...*you* know?"

"Know what?"

That made everyone laugh nervously, while Cecilly's face took on a temporary flush of color. As Patty jumped to the floor, Cecily stammered, "Like, I didn't know he was *real* when we did it...you don't think he could, like, have a disease, do you? Like AIDS? I mean, if he—if I got—"

Katie was a biology major, with hopes of becoming a medical student ("Where there are real men in the classroom, too," she'd often say over morning coffee) and she said, "I suppose it would depend on who he'd been with before you, but then vampires aren't human, so maybe the virus couldn't live in the undead... geeze, I don't *know*—"

"Couldn't it have been a dream? You could have scratched yourself while dreaming—" Leslie was taking a psych course and thought she was a baby Freud. Katie peered at the twin holes and said, "Puncture wounds. Can't do that with fingernails...not even those fake things you wear, Leslie."

Before the two girls began to test whether real or false nails could rake up a face better, Cecilly, shivering under her peach and ivory lace Teddy (which showed pale ghosts of her nipples and mons through the shimmering fabric) said "Does this mean I'm going to be a vampire, too? I don't like going outside at night!"

Patty thought that one over a second, and said, "Holy water should do it, if you put it directly on the wound...at least that's what the books say. But the books are about fictional vampires, they aren't supposed to be 'how-to' books. But the chapel should be open—*wait*—"she smacked herself on the forehead with the flat of her palm—"all we have to do is put a cross on it. If Cecily starts to smoke and burn then it's a real vampire bite—"

Indignant in her Teddy, Cecily said, "Nobody is going to burn me!"

"But we don't want you lurking around, nipping us every night," Elizabeth had piped up, and before Cecily could protest further, Jeanie took off her dainty gold cross necklace and as the other girls pinned Cecily against the cold white sink, Jeanie pressed the tiny cross right on the pair of small holes and....

Nothing happened. The holes were still there, true, and when they let go of Cecily (her nipples stood out like tiny marble rose-buds, pushing the thin lacy covering up and out) she was angry at them, but not frothing at the mouth over the indignity of facing the cross. Patty was stumped. Katie put some peroxide on the holes; they only bubbled a little, but the surrounding flesh didn't seem terribly infected. Leslie asked if Cecily could have been sleepwalking and jabbed herself with something but otherwise the rest of the girls took the scene with bored equanimity. Cecily did have a flair for the dramatic, what with her fancy, filmy little lace under-things, and swirling Gunney Sax style dresses, and bat's wing mascara...yet, if a vampire *was* fluttering around at night, Cecily would be a most likely target, with her long wavy hair and creamy skin. Perhaps, as Elizabeth told the other girls over lunch (at the Miranda Hawthorne's Young Ladies College, freshmen ate at their own table) this wasn't the type of vampire found in Patty's horror novels; perhaps he was a *good* vampire. Patty shook her head over the plate of spinach salad, but the others were intrigued, and urged Elizabeth to go on.

Somewhat self-consciously (she was, after all, a math major) Elizabeth said, "Well, maybe he just doesn't want blood, but... let's suppose he's the loving sort of fellow, maybe before he became a vampire he was a very sexy, sensual sort of guy, and likes that part of it the best. So what better place to go than here? It isn't as if we're all going steady and are getting it every night...."

"We can't even go with each other, like it really *mattered* among adults," Heather cut in, shredding a leaf of spinach in frustration. Nineteen heads nodded around the long table, while, seemingly more far off than it really was, the upper-classmen's tables rang with satisfied, complacent laughter and chatter. Although none of the girls said it at the time, each thought, *He wouldn't be appreciated with* them, *in the other dormitories.* Gradually, during the classes between lunch and the final meal of the day, the girls in the freshman class came to the conclusion that maybe, just maybe, their vampire was a good one, the kind who only wanted to spread a little cheer as payment for the blood he so tenderly took from them. Warming to that thought, Elizabeth told herself during advanced algebra, *It isn't as if I'm not in need of some cheering up myself,* then, remembering Cecily's straining nipples, and Heather's plate of mercilessly shredded spinach, she added to herself over a Ven diagram, *And I'm sure the others wouldn't mind some* cheer, *either.*

Over supper (Cecily's hand kept caressing her scarf-covered neck) they talked about "their" vampire; figuring out where he might "rest" (everyone knew that there were bats up in the tool-shed by the horse stables, as well as in—ironic touch—the bell tower of the chapel), deciding that he must have sensed a need in the freshman dormitory ("I know, Leslie, he heard your vibrator!" "Did *not!*") and, over dessert, unanimously deciding (weird diseases or not; after all, science comes up with vaccines for everything sooner or later) that *if* he were to come again, they would not resist....

He had come again. The girls had made no special preparations, other than leaving the windows open (the ancient building lacked screens; if you wanted fresh air, you paid the price when occasional mosquitoes came in) and making sure that they wore their best, most sensuous nightwear, yet the next morning, Heather had sauntered slowly into the bathroom, and, without a word, stood there, hand pulling the fine yellow hair away from her neck, waiting until all eyes were upon her. This time, the questions they asked took a different tack.

"Was...*it* cold, too?" (This from Cecily, who should have remembered.)

"No, not really, but he wasn't, y'know, *hot*, either...."

"Did he kiss you, too?"

"*Every*where I wanted." (Giggles over that, and more than one pair of damp panties.)

"Did he *say* anything?"

"No, Patty, and I didn't have time to ask anything, either!"

'Did he cast a *shadow*? Leslie asked sarcastically, with a

glance at Patty.

Moving over to the nearest sink (vampires or not, Heather still cast a reflection, as did Cecily in her matching skimpy pink bra and panties) Heather prodded the skin around her wound and said, "We were too busy for me to *notice*." Then, she said to Cecily alone, "Did he—" as she leaned over and whispered something in the other girl's ear.

Cecily blushed as pink as her underwear and nodded emphatically, then put her lips in Heather's mane of hair and began to whisper something which made Heather squeeze her legs together and exclaim, "Did he *ever!*" At that point, the others slowly left the room.

From that day on, Heather and Cecily were constant seatmates at meals, and soon their exclusive ranks were augmented by Jeanie (who wore her cross at night by mistake and *still* was visited, prompting Leslie to chirp, "Maybe he's an atheist vampire, huh?"), then Carol, and Patty herself, who merely said the next morning after her turn, "You can't believe *everything* you read in books."

A couple of days went by when no one made a dramatic showing in the dormitory bathroom, and the tension grew heavy among the sixteen "unchosen" as each wondered, *Will he come back? Were they the only ones he wanted?* Leslie joked that maybe he had found himself a desperate sophomore or an ugly senior, but the trouble was, the upperclassmen were, to a Young Lady, all reasonably good-looking, fairly popular girls, none of whom could easily be called "loose" or a "dog."

On the evening of the second day without his coming, Leslie said, "Maybe Patty did him in, y'know, maybe he got bookwormitis—"

Patty almost forgot she was a Young Lady and tried to deck Leslie from across the table and over the roast beef. Her sisters in new-vampirism held her back, and she grumbled, "You should just be that lucky."

As it turned out, Leslie *was* the lucky one that night...as, in a way, was Elizabeth. The beds in the dormitory were about five feet apart, ten beds facing each other on opposite sides of the room, with a nightstand between each bed, and two beds having nightstands that were against a wall. The group closets were along the other walls, except for where the doors going to the hallway, and their bathroom were. Leslie had one of the beds which was last in line, with only a nightstand between the bed and the wall. Elizabeth's bed was next to Leslie's, and on that particular September night, there was a full moon which shone in, making the room only semi-dark. Elizabeth gradually became aware that the bed-frame next to hers was wiggling, squeaking slightly, and after taking a quick glance over at Paula in the other bed near hers (she was curled up in a ball, back to Elizabeth), she quickly turned her head and looked at Leslie's bed...and the first thing that went through her mind was, *There's no shadow...none at all*, as she watched Leslie's shadow on the wall near her bed seemingly ride up and down, legs wrapped around nothingness....

Elizabeth was too shy to actually look at him, but she couldn't help but catch a quick glimpse of him (dark, *so* dark) and the brief look was more than enough, and until she fell asleep, she lay there eyes shut tight, ears straining to catch the slightest sound, the most tender caress of satin-covered flesh...and as she lay there, listening (*He whispered something to her, I heard it*), a plan began to form in her mind.

However sensual their vampire was, he wasn't predictable. He had left them high and dry for two days, waiting and eventually fighting over who, if *anyone*, would be next. And by now, the fear of him *not* coming (pun not anticipated, *but*....) was greater for the girls than the fear of actually doing *it* with a vampire, an undead being, a thing that slept hidden in the earth, or swinging by his feet, hidden among the rest of the icky, leathery *bats* on campus. By now, this had become a "chosen" and "unchosen" type of situation, more important and powerful than the old playground power-play of who gets chosen First and Last for kickball, who Makes or Doesn't Make the cheerleading squad, or even the up-coming worry of Sorority Rushes. *This* situation was different, more important. Something beyond them, beyond their petty *cliques* and imposed social orders was at play here, and all of them were under its spell. Suddenly, sporting a pair of tiny holes on one's neck was *the* thing which separated the Girls from the Women, the In from the Out. Even cynical, cool, soon-to-be-a-shrink *Leslie* wasn't immune from this. Even she had sat, chewing on the inside of her cheek when she thought no one was looking, no doubt wondering, *Why hasn't he come for* me?

Elizabeth knew what Leslie had been thinking from personal experience. She, too, had felt her panties grow damp while she thought about *him*, and wondered if tonight would be the magic time, the unthinkable moment. And she, too, had woke up and padded into the bathroom to stare at her harshly-lit reflection, and wonder why it didn't happen, again. At least, when it came to *real* men, a girl had a chance, even of being rejected. But to not be *considered*....

Elizabeth tried to act surprised when Leslie began to jump and down in front of a mirror, her bare feet smacking on the cold green tile floor below, her small breasts rising and falling under her white camisole. Leslie was soon surrounded by her "sisters" in carnal vampirism, and by now the other girls knew better than to ask questions. They had enough details for a thousand fantasies...but Elizabeth had an ace the other players weren't aware of. While not actually having had the real experience, she had been only five feet from it. And her hearing was excellent.

After appearing for five more days (Paula, while Elizabeth slept, then Katie, and Chris, then Lisa followed by Erika) their elusive Romeo was gone for a week, then two, then the first quarter was long gone, and keeping the windows open even a crack became uncomfortable (Leslie suggested that maybe they should nail them shut, since "It's too cold for *bats* anymore," and Elizabeth wished that Patty would have clawed her up, like in the good old days) in the Minnesota fall, yet the "unchosen" few would religiously prop the old windows open, and carefully put on their best finery each night after brushing their teeth.

But the unlucky nine woke each morning, looking and feeling in vain for those coveted little holes. Apparently, their vampire was a one-night stand; the eleven "chosen" never spoke of a repeat performance, but they weren't complaining, either. Even after their wounds closed, they still had *had* them, and during seemingly unrelated conversations between "chosen" and "unchosen" freshmen, whenever a "chosen" girl wanted to score a point, all she had to do was finger her neck....

Elizabeth kept mulling over the plan she had come up with during the night he was with Leslie; sometimes she told herself that it was silly, childish, yet other times (when a "chosen" girl would gently finger a spot on her neck and give Elizabeth a sad little smile) she thought that it would be worth it, worth the pain of possibly being found out, exposed as a liar. Sometimes, anything was better than being an "unchosen"....

She had picked a night exactly seventeen days since Erika was visited. Waiting until she could hear the other girls breathing quietly, she slipped out of bed, stepping swiftly across the oak floor in her bare feet, then she carefully turned the knob and entered the dormitory bathroom, where (in keeping with the prison-like atmosphere) the lights above the mirrors were never shut off, then closed the big, darkly-stained door behind her, so that as little light as possible escaped during her entrance. If anyone woke up and found her in there, she could always say she had to go to the bathroom...actually, she *had* to do that first, the cold floor of the dormitory and the bathroom (open windows didn't help in that regard!) make her bladder begin to ache.

Once she was done with that, she padded over to the nearest mirror, and extracted something from a handkerchief she had wadded up and hidden in the panties of her baby-dolls. The seam-ripper had its own case, and with trembling fingers (partly from the coldness shooting up through her bare feet into her body, and partly from fear of being caught) she pried it off, almost slicing her thumb in the process. Finally, the uncovered seam-ripper, two curved blades shining in the bright glare of light above her, was in her right hand; the hand she slowly brought up to her throat as she arched her neck backwards, praying to no one in particular that she wouldn't pierce her jugular...wherever that was on her neck.

And brought the twin blades in contact with her neck, and, after a split-second's hesitation, plunged them in.

* * * * * * *

The next morning, the squeal of delight coming from the freshmen girls' dormitory could be heard halfway across the campus. He was back! He had come! Elizabeth was surrounded by the others, the rest of the "chosen," and for the rest of the day, she had to rehash her "experience," and she was glad that she had had the foresight to plan out her story and run it through her mind a few times in the dim hours between the time when she did it and the time when the rest of the girls got up. Giving them all the juicy details over morning coffee and cocoa made it actually seem so real, and with each retelling, the images, the sounds, the sensations and the smells intensified in her mind, until a part of her did believe that he had come for her. She had thrown away the bloody seam-ripper, hence it didn't exist anymore...anyway, if she hadn't seen what she did with Leslie, she would have been content with her fantasy, since it was so vivid, so satisfying (and disease-free) and so nearly real. It had been like copulation with every man of her dreams, be he real or a flickering image up on a movie screen, doing every secret little thing she had ever dreamed that a man would do to her, and as she told her "sisters" about it, she knew that they believed her. Why wouldn't they? After she told her tale, each girl in turn told Elizabeth about *her* time with him—the fondled, kissed breasts, the flickering tongue in soft places, the cool, dry hands rubbing and exploring, the legs wrapped around his caped darkness (So *it wasn't a dream, I* did *see that!*) and soon the Dozen had damp panties and aching places once again and Elizabeth tried not to look too condescendingly at the Eight others, since she knew what it was like on their side of the fence, too.

* * * * * * *

It is a fact, not provable in all instances, but a fact nonetheless, that when a barren couple adopts a child, suddenly the tree might bear fruit and soon one child will become two...the next morning, it was Val's turn to prance around the cold green-tiled bathroom, to be coddled and admired, and Elizabeth had to stop herself from looking in the bottom of the trash bin, under the paper towels and neatly bagged used napkins, to see if there was a used seam-ripper, or a big safety pin, or something now bloody and sharp. But then, there was always the chance that he really did come back. If Elizabeth's ruse had done the trick, so be it. If not, did it really hurt anything to let Val have *her* fantasy, too?

So they became the Baker's Dozen, and the Seven dutifully marching to classes in silence, and if they doubted, they kept their doubts to themselves. Two days, three, passed and he did not return, if return he had done in the first place.

Elizabeth wondered why the others didn't think of doing it, of scampering on bare feet into the harsh world of the tiled bathroom and ugly old fixtures, sharp thing in hand, neck arched, waiting for the sharp swift pain, and then recalled something someone (it may have been herself, for that matter) had said after Cecily, something about him sensing a need in the girls, and giving cheer in return for taking their blood? Maybe the others didn't have the same need, or there was too much fear wrapped up around their need for him to be able to do them much good. But as she plotted a Venn diagram in class, she told herself, *That's* silly. *You needed it as much as the next woman, but he still didn't come for you. Maybe he's just selective...which doesn't say much about me, does it?*

But a memory of something she'd seen a few days ago, during the morning showers, made her wonder if the vampire wasn't able to pick up on their actual needs, and respond to them. Cecily had been talking to her as they put on their make-up over the sinks, and while she was trying to follow Cecily's conversation, she saw something happening in the shower area behind her (the showers were Dachau-like fixtures set along a back wall, with only a curtain to separate that part of the room from the rest of the bathroom, and no privacy between shower-heads), the curtain wasn't totally closed, and through the steam and rush of water, she thought that she could see two of the Seven "unchosen" ones soapily fondling each other, looks of bliss on their faces; then Cecily asked her something, and by the time she looked back in the mirror, someone had pulled the curtain shut. But she was sure that Nancy and Elaine were getting along just fine in there, *no*-petting-with-classmates rule or not. Looking back upon the incident, Elizabeth wondered if the vampire had avoided those two because they wouldn't welcome his cool embrace? Sure, they had taken part in the nightly dress-up parade, had expressed disappointment when they awoke with unblemished necks, but were they really all that sad about it?

And for that matter, was Elizabeth? Hadn't she pressed a cotton ball soaked in peroxide on her self-inflicted cut after making it? *Leslie* hadn't raced out of bed afterward to go and put peroxide on *her* real bite, and who knew what those teeth had bitten into lately?

Yet, despite the germs, Elizabeth had wanted the vampire to come to her, to touch and explore her body, to take so little in return for so much, to whisper "You are *mine!*" in her ear, like he did to Leslie (and supposedly) did with Erika and Val, to do what he would with her...and yet, now that she was counted among the "chosen," she was strangely content. And she wasn't like Nancy and Elaine; she had no urges to squeeze soapy pink flesh and rub a hair-rounded vulva, and didn't even worry when-ever one of the others gave her body the eye. Other people's fantasy lives were none of her business, and as long as they kept their hands to themselves—no, she wasn't unsure enough of herself to worry about being gay, as if that was something to *really* worry about. On the other hand...she was still a virgin, but that was by choice, even before her parents convinced her to go to college *here*. So, for the time being, she had put the matter from her mind and concentrated on her mathematics....

* * * * * * *

As she lay in her bed, tense and flowing under the covers, Elizabeth saw *him*, in his animal state, fluttering and flapping in furry darkness outside the window, his tiny body casting weird rippling shadows on the filmy white curtains. The windows (only a couple in the room, because of the cold) were open but a couple of inches...just wide enough for a small bat to wiggle through. Once the bat had passed through the narrow opening, it parted the curtains across from her, and instead of flying across the room to her bed, the bat began to grow, to lose its animal shape, becoming amorphous, spreading up and down in the darkness, at times so sheer she could see the moonlight through him, and other times he was a velvety, solid mass. The *sound* of him...like fur being rubbed against silk, a smoothly sensuous, utterly *warm* sound/sensation that made the fine hairs on her arms and upper thighs lift then settle gently. Noiselessly, he walked toward her bed, and under the covers her hands were rhythmic and steady, not missing a beat...then stopped when he stood next to her, his back to Leslie in her bed. Under the covers, Elizabeth lay spread-eagled, ready for him, looking into his darkness, his eyes which carried a light of their own...and as he stared at her, Elizabeth felt her *need*—and understood it, *fully*, for the first time.

I need the fantasy that I can control, not the reality I can't direct or anticipate...and in that moment, with the reality so close at hand, with the vampire standing by her, ready, she knew that no matter what *he* did, it could never be what she'd want done to her, even if she tried to tell him what she wanted. Something might get lost in the telling...something that she might *need*.

Her need understood, the vampire reached down, down, and before he did bite her throat (he was, after all, in need himself), he whispered in a breath flavored with a hint of earth, a touch of copper, and an underlying smell of something not unlike *herself,* "I know when I'm needed...and when I'm not. You are now a 'chosen' in reality...*your* reality, *your* way."

Closing her eyes while he briefly satisfied his need, she did not watch him depart from her unmolested body, did not see him fly away unspent and unmissed. When he was gone, her hands slowly slid around under the covers until they found the places of need. Slipping slowly towards dreams, Elizabeth and the vampire spent the rest of the night in the most leisurely, careful lovemaking imaginable by mortal woman, and Elizabeth decided *not* to mention the return visit to her roommates.

Her vampire didn't approve of making other people jealous. He was, after all, a gentleman.

AFTERWORD

This was the first vampire story I wrote, back in 1986 (it was published in 1987), hoping to do something in one of the traditional horror genres, but somehow it didn't quite work for the straight-on horror markets. I sent it to Peggy Nadramia of the late, lamented *Grue*, and she liked it, but didn't think it was a "Grue" story. But she did know of another editor, Alayne Gelfand, who was starting up a vampire magazine which would eventually become *Prisoners of the Night*, a publication which was perhaps a tad ahead of its time, what with the current popularity of vampire/romance-romance/vampire stories/novels. Back in the eighties, it was considered an "adult" magazine, and marketed more or less as such.

Now when it comes to the major horror themes (vampires, werewolves, ghosts, zombies *et al.*), I'm not all that into vampires *per se*...but that hasn't stopped me from writing enough erotic vampire stories to literally fill an erotica e-book! I do think that this story prefigures my interest in non-traditional vampires; a decade later I did a slew of erotica for Circlet Press that centered around cultural-variant vampires, plus I did a very non-erotic pair of regional-themed vampire stories for a couple of anthologies in the 1990s (collected elsewhere).

What does set this story apart, at least for me, was that it was included in Poland's first anthology of translated horror fiction published after the fall of Communism...only, I didn't realize that I was even in the book until years after it was published. My former European agent was in hock due to some gambling debts, so he stole the commissions from select reprints from his client, including my payment for the Polish reprint of "Of Vampires...." After his activities were discovered, the Science Fiction Writers of America (SFWA) had one member, Dave Smeds, track down all those people who'd been bilked, and notified them of the sales overseas. He initially secured a photocopy of my story from the anthology, then was later able to find a second-hand copy of the actual book, which he was kind enough to send to me. The story was also part of my Romanian-language collection *Femia Coperta* (*Cover Woman*) which was published in 2004; that collection was a mixed bag of horror, fantasy and sf, along with this bit of erotic horror, and was both translated and brokered by my long-time pen-pal Petru Iamandi. It was a lovely-looking collection, and has since sold out over there.

And just this last year, when I finally was able to reconnect with my father's side of the family, I found out that I'm actually one-eighth Polish (also one-eighth Russian, and one-quarter German).

So, all in all, a nice history behind this story, more or less....

"...AND THE HORSES HISS AT MIDNIGHT"

"Sure you've heard of *that* one," Mona the Tattooed Girl told me as she slipped her vine-covered fingers into my shirtfront. In the busy near-silence of the approaching nightfall, I heard one of the buttons give way and softly roll off into the trampled grass behind the midway, the sound all but lost in the swell of crickets and the distant tire-kisses on the highway far beyond.

Tracing the swell of one halter-trapped breast with my left hand, as my right wound around her bat-and-vine-encircled waist, I whispered once again, "No, I've never heard of snakes hiding in carousel horses...."

Another of my shirt buttons was liberated from the surrounding fabric before Mona replied, "But they do...it's only the people who don't believe who say it's untrue. The people who don't dare believe"—another pair of fingers sliding down my chest, another button rolling off to be forever lost in the litter-flecked grass—"and the people who are *afraid* to believe...."

"Why would they hide in wood?" My right hand slid downward, to her needle-embroidered belt with the navel buckle, lingering at that delicate indentation before seeking the softer, far deeper indentation below.

Mona's lips brushed against my chest a moment before she spoke against my skin, "Not in the wood itself...they hide in the cracks in the wood, the places hidden by the shadows and contours of the horse's surface...places you don't normally look. But just because they aren't seen, doesn't mean they aren't *there*." The last was almost muffled by my own quickly rising chest. My breath was coming in hitches. I let my hand wander across her back to fumble with the knotted ties of her halter as I asked her, "But why be there if no one sees them? What's the point in living just to hide?"

The Tattooed Girl's eyes glittered in the almost-full moonlight; her lipstick shone near-black against her small white teeth as she stared at me in the darkness. "'*What's the point*'—That's like saying what's the point in me getting all of these"—she used her button-popping hand to point to her embellished breasts and flatly-decorated torso—"If I don't walk around all but naked all the time...which I *don't*," she added defensively, and for a moment, I feared I'd lost my chance with her, the chance I'd been all but praying for since I'd first seen her earlier that evening, standing on her small stage in the Fabulous Freaks tent on the midway.

The "Freaks" part may have been something of a misnomer; the best this carnival could come up with was the ubiquitous Headless Woman sitting light-bulb-surmounted in her wooden chair, the parabolic mirror which hid her head *almost* flawlessly set up and lit, along with a merely anorexic-looking Thin Man and mediocre sword-swallower who used no sword thicker than a good-sized shish kebab holder. But "Fabulous" more than applied to the spot-lit Mona the Tattooed Girl. I thought, upon seeing her, that the word should've been forever reserved for her alone.

Spread-wing bats flapped with each languid exhalation and inhalation, all but flitting from bloody thorn to moon-kissed leaf. Kudzu vines seemed to grow upon her red-tipped fingers, winding and spreading over and around her knuckles, growing denser by the second. The arabesques encircling her arms and neck crept up onto the bare sides of her head, touching the roots of her shaggy dyed-blond Mohawk before winding upon themselves and snake-trailing down her spine, down to the low-slung waistband of her high-cut shorts. Sylphids and shaggy satyrs chased each other down and around her thighs, around each rose-touched knee, and spiraled down her calves to her flatly-bracleted ankles. Below the links of yellow-gold sank into her flesh, branching thinner chains of ink and imagination, leading down to her red-tipped toes. Only her face was free of permanent embellishment; her kohl-lined green eyes and glittering carmine lips had been decorated by her own hand. But the color in her cheeks which bloomed and flushed when she read my silently mouthed *Will you make love to me?* was perhaps the most wonderful, thrilling adornment on her entire ornamented body.

And more wonderful still, she was waiting for average, unadorned *me* after the carny wound down, after the wooden carousel horses did their last prance and canter before resting still and frozen in the moonlight. Taking my sweating, naked-looking fingers in her own cool vine-wound ones, she led me to a place of undisturbed grass and near-silence, her long mythic legs scissoring beside me...but before we could undress, before the promised lovemaking could begin, she'd whispered a strange thing about the horses, and the hidden snakes—

Hoping to recapture her ardor, or whatever it was that made an exquisite being like her blush and then mouth "Yes" to my request for sex (was it my use of the word "love" that had swayed her, or did she find my mundane exterior somehow exotic in its ordinariness?), I reached up and caressed the smooth side of her head, then moved my fingers and thumb close to her eyes, her lips, and said, "All right, all right, so they live *to* hide...maybe they want to, or like to?"

That brought back her smile, made her dancing eyes glitter. "Yesss," she said in a rush of warm air against my gently probing fingers, "that's what they like best of all...the coming out *after* hiding...." Closing her eyes until her lashes cast fluttery crescents across her upper cheeks, she reached behind her and undid her halter ties herself, but allowed me the honor and pleasure of removing the twin triangles of black fabric. Revealed in the moonlight, her nipples and breasts cast small shadows on her flesh; both fleshy protrusions were decorated right up to the very tips of the nipples with petal after layered petal—each breast was a full-blown chrysanthemum surrounded by curling rings of leaves.

Closing my eyes for a moment, I could almost feel the individual petals beneath my delicately tracing fingers, but Mona reached up and thumbed both my eyes open, then let her forefingers linger on my temples. Rubbing them gently, she whispered, "Time for botany later...they wait until they're being ridden, before coming out, y'know," she went on dreamily, as she moved her hands down my cheeks and neck, her flesh gliding smoothly, like slick leaves, until she'd reached my chest, and nipples.

Circling my flesh with her thumbs, Mona shifted slightly below me as if trying to squirm out of her cutoffs without touching them with her hands, as she went on in that same lazy yet succinct voice, "It's best when there's a child, or a woman on the horse...that's when the snakes slither out of the cracks, one by one, and inch by inch, and when there's a little bit of silence between the notes of the carousel, they start to hiss...maybe one at first, then a couple of them, hiss *hiss*...and while they're doing that, they undulate, maybe touching the rider's calf, or a kneecap...whatever's exposed, whatever's *unsuspecting*—"

Finally taking her nonverbal hint, I reached down and began to undo the buttons under the fly of her cutoffs, wanting to pop the buttons off as she had done to me, but still afraid to be so rough, so obvious. This was her place, her world, and I didn't know who might come running should she cry out or worse.

"—and maybe at first they think it's a bug, or some part of their clothes that's loose and flapping, but then, when the snake's little tongue does that slow flicker and snap-back, *then* the rider knows...and *then* the rider hears the hissing for what it is, but the ride is going 'round, y'know? It can't stop...there's no emergency brake on a merry-go-round," she added with this little chuckle that never reached her staring eyes. Mona waited until my fingers had freed the last of the buttons before wrapping both arms around my back and whispering in my ear, "So the rider just goes 'round and 'round, while the snakes slither up and around their little knees and feet, hissing and waving, enjoying the ride...and all the rider can do is grab hold of the pole and scream against the music...and the ride goes so fast, no one else can see the snakes...'specially not the other people on the ride, the ones whose snakes are hiding for now—"

Hitching my fingers into her waistband, I waited until Mona arched her back slightly before tugging down the shorts. Once they were past her hips, her knees, she wiggled until they could be kicked off her body with her lower legs...and as she was busy freeing herself of the cutoffs, she relaxed her grip on my body just enough so that I could get a good moonlit look at what was tattooed beneath the place where her shorts had been—

That she was bare down there was a given; hadn't she told me earlier that she was going to get rid of her Mohawk, add more snaking swirls and geometric designs on her very skull? But I had to blink my eyes a few times to register what I saw tattooed on and around her gently mounded mons and swollen labia—the second set of carmine lips and sharply outlined, tattoo-crosshatch-shadowed teeth surrounding her lower set of lips, the colored twin curve of the *faux* carmine-inked lips glistening, as if she'd just licked them moist. I reached down to probe and caress that second waiting mouth, but what I felt only confused me more. The lips seemed to pucker against my flesh, as if to kiss my fingertips, while just beneath them I felt the hardness and rounded smoothness of teeth—some of them sharply pointed. I longed to probe deeper, to touch her hidden depths and moist inner pools, but to do so, I'd have to risk passing those teeth. Something as dangerous as it was unexpected...yet something enticing, because it *was* so out of the ordinary.

I started to speak, to question, but Mona shook her head, the thick swath of silver curls in the middle rippling against the grassy ground under her skull. "Ride's started," she whispered, "No emergency brake, remember?" Wrapping her legs around me, trapping my swelling organ against my undershorts, Mona snaked her right arm down my back and dug her thumb under my waistband until she could pull my jeans and underwear down close to my hips, then lower...and she hugged me against her as the snap and zipper let go, and the last of the entrapping, protective fabric pulled free of my lower body. She was hissing in my ear, "I won't bite it *off*...but don't be surprised if you feel a tiny pinch down there...remember the snakes, how they love to flick their tongues. And the snakes only come out when the ride's going 'round, so be ready to get off once the music's over...."

I could have left her then, before it began, but no other ride at this carnival promised so much, even as it so openly threatened me. Even the horses with their hidden snakes seemed tame in comparison with what Mona was offering me, and me alone—

—and so as she pulled me closer and deeper, I felt a brief, slick hardness as I slid into her. The ridges of the longest, sharpest teeth barely grazed my incoming flesh, but true to her word, those teeth never bore down on me. She began to hum softly, a lilting drone that swelled in my ear...and I never got to ask her what the consequences of lingering too long in that tightly warm elastic-walled mouth might be once that melody reached its unexpected end, for the ride had indeed begun, and since there was no stopping, I felt compelled to keep up my own dizzying rhythm while my own lips explored her face and breasts, even as her nether lips explored and sucked deeply on my own imprisoned flesh.

Perhaps she sensed the throbbing in my lower back, a pain barely perceptible through my steadily growing orgasmic haze. Perhaps she sensed the gradual slowing up of the rhythm between us, a union of motion matched to her melodious murmuring. Perhaps...she sensed that the snakes longed to be hidden once more. Pushing me up and safely out of her, she abruptly stopped the song, just as I felt a teasing, yet definite nip close to the base of my now slippery organ (accompanied by a deep sucking pull on the pinched flesh). The heretofore melody-masked sound of crickets and highway movement came flooding back against my eardrums. Like a snake shedding its skin, my member shrank and rested as if satisfied against my now-dangling testicles. A glistening black pearl-like drop of blood welled up from the spot where I'd been bitten. *"Ride's over, time to get off."* And like the stilled-in-motion carousel horses, Mona's sated set of *faux* tattooed lips grew flatter and less detailed as they and the teeth below sank back into a pool of inky color and detail against her still moist flesh. Soon only a fine dribble of her own saliva-like juices remained near the natural pucker of her labial lips, as if waiting for a good-bye kiss....

I don't know if she comprehended my last caresses, my last lingering, tongue-probing kisses above and below; only by the slight rise and fall of her nightmare-bloom bedecked rib cage and breasts could I tell she was even alive. Her flushed eyelids were closed, but whether she slept or whether she was merely reliving recent pleasures, recent meals, in the darkened confines of her mind, I could not tell. She was just silent.

But...what *was* there to say, or to ask? I doubted she'd answer any of my questions, even if she could. Even if she knew, telling would only spoil her dark, exotic magic for me. Like probing tiny cracks and crevices of the carousel horses for hidden snakes before the music and the motion began...or like pulling aside her clothing *before* she's mouthed that magical "Yes" of assent. To have done that would've spoiled the surprise, ruined that pleasure which comes with the gradual revelation *after* hiding and hinting. I could never ask her which came first, the snakes with their teasing tongues, or the tattooed lips and barely grazing teeth, for both were as intertwined as they were unique, one forming the echo to the other's sound, or the shadow to the form....Enough that she'd shared *her* own hidden "snakes" with me...and had asked so little in payment for the ride.

I gathered up my clothes and threw them on, alternately peeking at her supine form and quickly looking elsewhere. Beyond, the rest of the carnies were busy taking apart the rides, the booths, and talking softly among themselves. None of them noticed me (or if they did, they knew better than to acknowledge my unofficial presence, perhaps remembering Mona's other rides, and other riders) as I darted, buttonless shirt flapping, through the last remainders of the midway, a rider perhaps *too* ordinary for comment despite what Mona had revealed—and done—to me.

The bite on my now-covered flesh still stung almost pleasantly with each step, even though *I* still seemed to be unchanged. I wondered if one of the carnies would come to fetch Mona from her sated slumber before morning came, provided someone *had* noticed us out there. But as I passed the carousel, its painted mounts air-suspended, hooved legs caught in mid-arc, I realized that my passing in Mona's domain hadn't gone entirely unnoticed—nor had my small payment for the ride left me unaltered, or *ordinary*:

Emerging from its hiding place for one daring, riderless second, a snake hissed at me from one of the suspended horses.

AFTERWORD

This is actually the second version of this story I've written; the first (which actually appeared a few years *after* the vampire version came out in a small press magazine called *Fortress*), was non-vampiric, but when I received an invitation from Poppy Z. Brite to submit a story to her upcoming vampire erotica anthology, I quickly rewrote it and sent it off to her. She suggested some changes, which I made, and afterward I sold the story. It later appeared in *The Year's Best Fantasy and Horror*, and between that original sale, the reprint sale, and many years worth of royalties, this particular tale ended up being my biggest individual money-maker. Too bad I didn't call it "...And the Cash Cows Hiss at Midnight"!!

The original version appeared in my now out-of-print collection *Smothered Dolls*, as well as in one of my upcoming (and as yet untitled) collections from Borgo—aside from the altered horror element, the beginning of that story is much more like the original beginning of *this* story, so those of you who want to see how the editorial process works can compare my text with Poppy's revisions.

The whole urban legend aspect of both versions had to do with my research into urban legends, for an anthology idea I was pitching to a well-known anthology editor—he passed on it, but an assistant of his took my research and ended up selling what was basically my idea to another publisher, cutting me and the anthology editor out of the loop. I don't know if it did well or not, but I do suspect it helped me to sell a later antho idea to the same antho editor, probably because his assistant had stolen my earlier idea.

Ironically, this sale to Poppy didn't lead to all that many horror antho sales, but within the decade I was regularly appearing in erotica anthos, under two pen names—I've actually done better under those names when it came to not only getting into anthos, but later getting into various erotica "Year's Best" anthos. Under my own name, I was only in the *YBF&H* series then edited by Ellen Datlow and Terri Windling, but my erotica has made it into three different editor/publisher's "Best Of" collections, plus one of the Circlet Press anthos (including a story of mine) was nominated for a Lambda Award.

Not bad for someone who has never even dated....

THE UPPYROAKE
KAMIKAZE AND THE
VIRGIN SHREDDER

During long winter nights in Fargo, when wind-driven snow comes scudding down the middle of the streets like sparkling silvery dust-devils, small tornado-shaped wraiths that dissolve in the bracing night air once they hit a car, or a quick-moving pedestrian, the last stop of the evening for the most...adventurous types is the karaoke show at Mc Cronan's, also known as Mc C's, or Sodom and Gomorrah of the High Plains. Don't bother trying to look it up in one of the city's various yellow pages, or the Chamber of Commerce listings. I don't even think it's part of the city's official website.

All you have to do is find the sort of people who come crawling out of their walk-up apartments, or single-wide trailers, or downtown squats only after the sun has slid on down past the flat horizon, ask "Where's the show?" and they'll point it out to you, if they're not too wasted—or weak—to lift a hand in the general direction. I suppose in the most superficial sense, Mc C's (as the regulars are wont to call it) shouldn't be called a karaoke bar at all, since most bars serve liquor, and this joint lost its license back in the days when "Paradise by the Dashboard Light" was still available on 8-tracks, and nobody had heard of tiny silvery disks called "cd's"....But much like its booze-fueled sister singing establishments, Mc C's is a very strange, very weird world unto itself...no, stranger and weirder than most, as

I've come to learn....

For starters, I don't believe that the typical karaoke kamikaze who frequents the usual k-bars each night, just salivating for the chance to belt out whatever scrolls across the twin TV screens in exchange for a free drink is anything like Zivon Adrikova... for, despite the fact that nothing with a bigger buzz than a Red Bull is served there, Zivon manages to drink his fill of a more personal intoxicant nightly—and without setting the manager back the price of a can of cola.

Once Zivon steps up on that stage, the color backgrounds of the monitors bathing his pale flesh in an undulating rainbow of oleaginous iridescence, all the karaoke chicks start panting open-mouthed, pressing tight against the apron of the stage, the ice in their hand-held drinks chittering and clicking against the surrounding glass like beetles fucking in an empty Mason jar. And when he opens his mouth—the whole bugs-screwing analogy heats up a few notches, to the point where all you'd need to do to melt the snow off the parking lot would be to toss every one of those ladies outside, rear-first....

And it doesn't matter if he's belting out vintage Al Green, or those Meat Loaf paeans to teen lust, or some tired groaner like "Feelings"—once his tight slash of a pale mouth opens, and those opalesque grey-blue eyes narrow at the corners as he strains to read the lyrics off the nearest TV screen, women go Defrost. As I well know.

Before the first time I saw Zivon do his thing, I'd never actually sat all the way through one of those shows, or paid much attention. Oh, I'd been in k-bars before, O'Leary's here in the city, a few others in the Twin Cities to the East. Usually, that fatigued *cliché* about having seen one means having seen them all (be it a k-bar, a woman's exposed chest down in New Orleans come bead-tossing time, or a guy's unzipped fly) applies to places like this, but thanks to Zivon, Mc C's went well beyond *different*. As I was soon to discover, the hard way.

But I'm swallowing before biting here—

First impressions: Without the aroma of spirits to quickly

numb one's nostrils (as well as mask the inevitable funk generated by too many bodies shoehorned into too small a space), I quickly picked up the scent of rut. Like hunting not with a rifle, ammo, and camo, but instead relying on half-unbuttoned shirts, butt-flossing thongs under short skirts, and plenty of mouthwash in pocket packs. No beer served meant no neon beer signs, just a few dim bulbs dotting the ceiling in distant constellations. A sense of unspoken tension, an aura of anticipation, no, more like hyper edginess, underlying the relative lack of chit-chat around me.

Nothing like the other k-bars I'd been in, where the crowd gets sucked into that pseudo-allure generated by a warm body standing alone on a bright-lit stage, no matter who was up there, or how horribly he or she sang (someone did tell me that a bad singer "shreds" a song, then quickly added that the crowd would listen to him or her caterwaul anyhow). There was someone on Mc C's stage when I first came in, but I doubt anyone there could've told me what the guy was singing had I asked them to help him read the lyrics off the monitors. Like I said, this anxious buzz—

Then the song (which even I can't recall) was over, and the man stumbled in the sugary semi-darkness off the stage—to be replaced by a thin, wiry young guy, maybe five ten-five eleven (in boots), his light brown hair way longer than was fashionable even in an out-of-the-loop place like Fargo, but curly enough to surround his head like a nimbus rather than brush his shoulders, with a face that would've looked more in place at an Oktoberfest or lutefisk feed—an obvious immigrant's face, easily at home (as in home country) somewhere in Scandinavia, or possibly Eastern Europe...broad brow, wide cheek bones, well-fleshed nose and chin, wide-set eyes—who made his way up the stairs to the stage. His clothes were a throwback to the swinging seventies—fringed leather jacket, jeans that were pleasantly tight in the butt but flared out at the ankles, worn buckled leather boots with at least an inch-high heel, and one of those super-shiny synthetic fabric pastel shirts which buttoned snugly across his chest, like someone had raided the costume departments of all the major studios in that decade, and merged the clothing worn by all the disco dons in *Saturday Night Fever* and that rabid squirrel of a serial killer from the first *Dirty Harry* movie. Between the clothes, and the man himself, the look was sexy in a feral sort of way, topped off with eyes that glittered just a little too brightly, and a mouth that obviously never smiled often enough.

Next to me, my old friend from high school, Ivan Yura, whispered "There be the *man*...wait'll you hear him. And just watch what the rest of the women do...." Ivan came here a lot (or so he'd told me during the drive to the outskirts of town earlier that evening), mostly to pick up some guy named Zivon's leftovers... as in all the chicks he couldn't possibly score with that night, but who still had jones's going on which wouldn't go away with the help of two fingers *or* a vibrator. Or so Ivan claimed.

So. This had to be Zivon. With an "i" not an "e" as Ivan corrected me when I'd made some admittedly lame Warren Zevon joke when we were in the car.

But Ivan had added just as we'd pulled into the parking lot, "This dude ain't no werewolf, but I think one of them Cheney guys played what he really is—"

I hadn't given Ivan's remark much more thought than it was due (after all, my old pal Ivan *was* the type of guy who would be lucky to score some karaoke kamikaze's sloppy seconds), but once Zivon centered himself in the middle of that small stage, the cast-off light of one monitor shining directly in his face, and the background monitor illuminating his tangle of curls in a nimbus of changing hues, he slowly leaned forward, cradling the head of the microphone in one thin-fingered hand, while his other hand curled around the stand itself in a not-so-overt priming-the-love-pump gesture parallel to his crotch, that growing sense of nervous anticipation surrounding me suddenly released, as if the entire room had just let out a deep, shuddering, collective sigh.

And when he lifted his head up, prior to opening his mouth

as the music swelled from the speakers surrounding him, all he had to do was look, really *look* into the audience before him, and we were all sucked in. Ivan and I were sitting maybe fifteen feet away, but those eyes of Zivon's were so glassy-bright, so intensely energetic, it felt as if their very gaze could smite my flesh, make the surface blister and crackle, even as I unabashedly loved every burning second of the pain—

And his voice was as harsh-yet-alluring as his all-encompassing stare—admittedly musical, but archly distant, with every syllable delivered with a crispness that bordered on the sadistically surgical even as the sheer melodic momentum of the tune managed to carry him through the song...which, as all things ironic, strange and yet oh so fitting would have it, was that boom-box-over-the-head rutting anthem, "In Your Eyes." And unlike the occasional half-watched singers from my past karaoke bar visits, Zivon didn't indulge in kariography—no swaying, no fake swooning in time to the music, no budging from his forward lunging pose, hands firmly positioned on that microphone. He didn't need to. By the second stanza, *we* were the ones doing the undulating, the rocking back and forth, drink-holding hands forming a frenetic icy descant to his relentless recitation of the unabashedly sexy lyrics in that cool-to-the-point-of-brittle-irony medium tenor voice of his.

I was squirming in my seat, unable to take my eyes off the oddly sexy-smarmy young man before me, when Ivan clumsily leaned over (and spilled at least half his glass of Diet Coke with Lime on my sweater-sleeve) and whispered in my left ear, his lips close enough to brush against the lobe, "You realize what he *is*, don'tcha? A bloodsucker. Calls himself a *yooopeir*—"

Painfully, I forced myself to look away from Zivon, and whispered back (avoiding *his* ear entirely), "He can't be a *yooper*...he's not one of those folks from the Upper Peninsula of Michigan, for crissakes. How's it spelled?"

"Look for yourself if he comes this way...it's carved on his damned chest—"

Damned if Ivan-the-Pitiful wasn't right. I could just make out the top of what looked like a capital "P" and possibly a "Y" in *bas-relief* against the top of his half-exposed chest, just parallel to the collar bones. And as if he realized that I was staring at him so intently, so purposefully, Zivon made his first seemingly extraneous movement—releasing the microphone stand, he ran his forefinger slowly down the front of his shimmering shirt, popping open a couple of buttons, so that his upper chest was fully exposed. Ivan was right, but he couldn't pronounce the word worth shit.

"UPYR"...a variant spelling on the modern Russian "*uppyr*," a much older spelling if my memory of a long-ago university course in vampire literature around the world was correct. The word wasn't carved into his skin, but appeared to have been branded there using a crudely-forged iron, perhaps fashioned solely for a single use—

And while I'd been deep in thought, the song came to an end, and even as the music died out, the sensations coursing through my body had yet to reach their peak—setting down my own glass of cola, whose ice cubes were still crashing against each other as well as the sides of the glass itself, I joined the others in applause, as Zivon curtly nodded toward us, and released the microphone. Before he'd quitted the stage, some other guy had taken his place, hoping perhaps to absorb some of the residual heat generated by Zivon's performance.

What that fellow sang, or sounded like, I have no idea to this day, for once Zivon reached the main floor of the packed room, he plunged through the sea of panting, leaning-towards-him female flesh...and didn't stop until he'd reached the small table Ivan and I shared. Up close he was far more shattering a presence than he'd been from five yards away. The branded scar on his chest was easily four inches tall and at least six wide, each letter raised above the surrounding skin just enough to cast a slight shadow around the edges, a fleshy *bas-relief*. Glancing down at his own chest for a moment, he pulled out one of the two empty chairs at the table, and said as he sat down next to me, "I guess I'm lucky they didn't use Cyrillic, aren't I?"

His speaking voice was as musically-harsh-yet-precise as his singing voice, but what was most jarring was his accent...pure High Plains, with that quasi-Canadian lilt which made most non-Dakota folks think people like us *were* Canadians.

Not what one would expect a vampire, or an *"uppyr"* to sound like at all—

(Around us, I was only vaguely aware that the other women were moaning softly in resignation, as if they knew that this would not be *their* night—something I'm sure Ivan was counting on when he brought me here. New meat and all—)

"Oh, I don't know about that...a lot of Russians settled here," I found myself saying, as if speaking to vampires (or guys who considered themselves to be vampiric) was part of my normal routine, but Zivon leaned forward, close enough for me to realize that his body was throwing off absolutely no heat whatsoever, and replied with a wink, "Not all of them are from the Ukraine... where they only use one 'p' in the word. But as long as the meaning's the same, someone out there will understand it. Or bother to look it up. Me, I'm just as happy they only heated up four letters, not five. Less painful, even if they did let me throw myself into the snow after they did it. They were so surprised, that I could feel pain like that—I think they were expecting me to burn up on the spot."

While he spoke, Zivon stared at me, not exactly undressing me with his eyes, but something far more intimate—watching my pulse points, where the blood thudded the strongest in my veins and arteries. And without having to ask, I knew what whoever it was had branded him was trying to do—exterminating vampires by fire was far more common in Russian vampire lore than even using the traditional aspen wood stake or disinterment, but as I thought about it, I realized that when Zivon was permanently marked for the rest of his un-dead existence, trees of any sort were scarce on the plains, so scarce that the nineteenth-century settlers might have had to use a more creative means of trying to kill off—or at the least, mark, their resident *uppyr*.

Allowing my eyes to stare into his, I felt a fiery sensation in my torso, my hidden sex, as the blue-gray irises of his wide-set eyes were eclipsed by blacker-than-moonless-midnight pupils, in whose reflection I saw tiny shimmering images of myself, vanishing into that ebony darkness. Reflexively, I reached out my hands as he extended his toward mine, and when our fingertips met, it was as if I'd made contact with textured ice, moving, dry, responsive ice that curled around my fingers and palm, and pressed cool and gentle against the insides of my wrists.

But as cool as he was to the touch, I didn't feel chilled at all—inside, I felt as if every vein and artery was surging with bubbling, boiling blood, blood that needed release, least it make me explode on the spot—and when he stood up, I moved upward along with him, and without really thinking, I walked along with him through the crowded bar, our legs brushing against chair legs and quickly retracted knees, and if anyone was still singing behind us, I couldn't hear it for all the rush of blood in my ears. I'd left my jacket hanging on the back of my chair, but I hardly needed it as Zivon and I pushed open the doors and walked out into the parking lot, our bodies shielded on all sides by sloppily-parked pick-up trucks and rust-filigreed beaters, My body was covered in a fine misting of white vapor—steam, from my burning skin meeting the February chill around me. But Zivon was unchanged, and when he breathed, no billow of white formed in front of his face.

Leaning with my back against the third door of a pick-up truck, I began to unbutton the top of my sweater-set, but Zivon shook his head of curly hair, and whispered, "Not the neck— too obvious, and too difficult to reach without hurting you. Just kiss me...I'll do the rest." When I was slow to respond, he leaned closer, and added softly, "*Trust* me." Up close, I could see that his incisors weren't anything like those of Hollywood vampires...he had smallish, even white teeth, from front to back, but in the moonlight, I could see how paper-cut-thin-and-sharp his front teeth were, their edges knife-straight and new-razor-blade keen....

Cupping the back of my head in his palm, Zivon gently guided my face close, closer to his own, until our lips were grazing skin against skin, then, he murmured, "Close your eyes" before opening his mouth and pressing it tightly against my own. The sensation of his lips, his tongue, his teeth, touching my own was glacial, piercing in its boreal intensity, even as I gradually felt the urgent pressure of his hands, his thrusting hips against my aching jeans-covered mound, his left knee pushing outward against my right, until my legs were spread open in welcome. Taking my right hand off his waist, I thumbed open my jeans button, and let gravity work the zipper down on its own. For his part, Zivon yanked open his own jeans, then pulled aside the leg-band of my boy-leg panties, before...I was entered by a chilly-but-exhilarating rigidness, a smooth fleshy stake that made my lower body tingle with deep shivers of undulating pleasure. And as my body's oily juices surrounded his deep-thrusting icicle-hard penis, I felt him grow warmer inside me, just as another sensation of warmth—hot-flowing, gushing liquid warmth—rushed into my mouth, and into Zivon's. The sensation of him slicing the inside of my lip with his teeth hurt no more than a paper cut might, and within seconds, his probing tongue-tip was massaging the sore spot, chilling my tender incised flesh, until the only sensation I felt throughout my body was one of numbing, blissful release, like the last moments of wakefulness before sleep overtakes one's body and mind, even as my senses remained sharp, razor-sharp and so utterly acute. While he thrust himself deeper into me, I straddled him with my legs, wrapping them around his hips.

The addition of my weight to his made no difference; each plunging forward motion was as deep and as satisfying as the first, and he didn't need to cup his hands under my behind to balance me against him, either.

It was...perhaps the most perfect act of lovemaking I'd ever experienced, a physical merging of two disparate bodies, one achingly hot, the other Siberian-cold, into one unifying whole. That I was literally giving of myself physically, on more than one level, was merely the starting point...for with each successive stroke, each absorbing pull of his mouth on mine, Zivon gradually—*ever* so gradually—took on some of my warmth, until I could actually feel hot breath against my cheek as he kissed me, and the lambent warmth of his hands as he caressed my back, my breasts. But I was so close to climaxing, my lower lips quivering against his now-burning member within me, that all I could do was melt against that unyielding truck door, allowing him to drain away the last lingering vestiges of my mortal resistance.

And when he climaxed, there was no sensation of semen flowing into me, but he still shuddered before growing softer within me, and as he pulled himself out of me, my legs went limp, and my boot soles hit the now snow-free parking lot with a rasping thud. Only then did he break the kiss, pulling his face from mine slowly, while his raised hands lingered on my waist and left breast. The sensation of the frigid night air hitting my numbed lips brought back the thin sliver of pain within my mouth, and I finally opened my eyes, to see Zivon staring at me, his glittering pale eyes moist with unshed tears.

"It won't hurt for long," he assured me, his voice softer than a sigh, as he helped me pull up my jeans, before he put his flaccid member back inside his own pants. In the moonlight, I saw the branded raised letters, now shiny in actual sweat on his chest, and noticed that his hairline also was dotted with moisture. Grabbing his hands before they moved from his crotch, I felt their smooth-textured surfaces, now damp with perspiration.

"Did *I* do this to you? Will it last?"

"I wish it could...but yes, you're feeling your warmth, in me. I...wouldn't exert myself, too much, at least not for a day or so. I took...more than I should've from you. Forgive me...I...lost control—" Zivon started to walk away from me, but I held his hands tightly, and pulled him back toward me.

"That...burn on your chest, they did that to you because of the sort of thing we just did? It's not just the blood with you, is it?"

Each time he breathed, the plume of white vapor coming

from his nose and mouth grew less visible in the moonlight, as if my stolen heat was moving quickly through his body, and dissipating with what might have been each heartbeat, had he been truly alive. And between my clasping hands, his own grew ever cooler, as he said, "No, it's not just the blood. Although that's how I feed, that's what nourishes me. I simply can't sneak up on someone and feed...I need to sing for my supper, as it were. An unfeeling...partner is useless to me. I have to make her want me, feel that intense heat for me, that fiery *need*... before I became as I am, the one thing about me which set all the young maidens aflame was my voice. Women have always loved to hear me sing. Why, I've no idea. I've heard my voice, the owner of this place once taped me, tried to play it when I was...otherwise engaged. But I had more women than I could handle coming out onto the parking lot, looking for me when I was..." here his voice grew sharply bitter, pitiful in its remorse, "feeding."

"Will this...make me as you are?" I don't know why I asked, I certainly was past caring, even if it were the case.

"I hope that it won't," he said with a trembling note in his voice, "And if you're as good a person as I suspect you are, you'll pray to whomever or what ever it is that you might believe in that it won't."

"Did a female...like you do this? To you?" Around us, the once melted surface of the parking lot was beginning to ice up, creating a silvery-bright mirror around us under the three-quarter moon above.

Unable to resist, I glanced down at that shining surface, and saw that Zivon *did* cast a reflection, but when I raised my eyes to his, he said, "You've got to stop thinking of my kind as being something out of that Stoker fellow's novel...besides, he was working off Romanian vampire lore. In Russia, things were a lot different."

Taking one of his hands out from between mine, he put his arm around my shoulder and helped me navigate across the slick icy asphalt, saying into my ear as we gingerly made our way back to the squat cinderblock club, "No one did...*this* to me but myself. Many, many years ago, someone I loved died, and all I could think of was how I wanted to be with her, as she was. So... against the laws of the gods and the will of the country, I killed myself. Only...she stayed dead, and I was soon something worse than dead. Most Russian *upir lichy* begin their undead existence as suicides. That is why they consider us to be wicked vampires. Because we *are* so much like living humans. We feed, we have needs, we cast reflections in mirrors. And other shiny surfaces," he added with a distinct smile in his voice, as we skidded up against the front entryway of Mc C's, our combined weight pushing us through the swinging door.

The inside of the club was actually darker than the moonlight chill behind us, but it wasn't murky enough that I wasn't able to make out my erstwhile escort, Ivan the Mediocre, attempting to sing up on that monitor-lit stage. I think he was slaughtering "Radar Love"—I could detect that familiar thump-thump-thump beat, but Ivan was so off-key, so relentlessly strident, it was truly difficult to be absolutely sure.

"Typical shredder," Zivon whispered into my ear, as he continued to hold onto my shoulder as we threaded our way through the flesh and wood labyrinth of customers, chairs and tables, until he and I reached the still-empty table where Ivan and I had first been sitting.

When I looked at him quizzically, he explained, "Someone who butchers a song, like your friend is doing. Apparently no one was desperate enough to go with him after I finished singing," and from the tone of his voice, I realized that Zivon in all likelihood was just as aware of Mc C's male clientele as he was of the distaff members of his nightly audience.

Since everyone else around us was talking quietly to each other, deliberately oblivious to Ivan's hair-tossing and gyrating "performance," Zivon and I spoke softly in each other's ears, as those who have so recently shared something so intimate are wont to do—especially in a club where something more traditional, like smoking off the same cigarette, was forbidden.

Taking my left hand in his, palm-down, he placed it across the branded patch of skin on his cool chest, and whispered, "*This* happened here, a century-and-a-half ago. When all you could see on the horizon was flatness dotted with the occasional rounded mound of a sod hut. I came here along with a group of Ukrainian immigrants, across the ocean in a horrid stinking boat...not daring to feed during the entire trip, lest I be found out for what I was. So—when I arrived here, I was famished, and unable to restrain myself. I looked as I do now, so the younger women, even the married ones, found themselves unable to resist me. I tried to be discrete, perfected my nearly invisible means of feeding without leaving such obvious markings on my...conquests' necks, but I became careless, and allowed myself to grow attached to one of my women, who in turn was all too willing to keep me well-fed, and warm during the coldest winter you can imagine, with virtually nothing to prevent the incessant winds from nearly slicing a body in two....I was found with her, and held prisoner in a "soddie" just long enough for the nearest blacksmith to create a special brand for me. The irony was, there were so few people and so much work which needed doing, they didn't wish to cast me *out*, but simply label me for what I *was*. I...suppose it was my gratitude to them, for not actually ending my existence, which has kept me in this place.

"Oh, I've ventured away from here; for awhile I serviced an entire Goth harem in Chicago, one of those vampire bars where *all* they do is slice and suck each other, but...they didn't want me to make love to them. Claimed it wasn't part of the 'true' vampire experience. And most of those women, despite their black lips and their shadowed eyes, and those chiffon and velvet tatters they wore, were actually good people, when not pretending to be vampires' women. Nothing like the *ereticy*, back in my homeland," he emphasized with a firm mashing-down of my palm against his *bas-relief* flesh. "Nothing like *them* at all."

"The '*ere...*'?" I let my voice trail off quizzically, as I ran my other hand along his cheek, relishing the lightly-stubbled coolness of his strong-boned face.

"*Ere-ti-cy*," he spat out fervently, loudly enough for some of the other people around us to turn in our direction, before going back to ignoring Ivan as he continued to screech between the monitors. "Women who did something worse than I did... they deliberately sold their very souls to the devil himself," he finished in a far softer tone of voice, close to my ear. "They slept in graveyards on the resting places of the unpious, when they weren't trying to turn men away from the true faith of our land. Sometimes, they ventured into bathhouses, the most male of enclaves, and begin making...noises. Unseemly cries, unbecoming any virtuous woman, or any mortal woman. Animal in heat sounds, yet irresistible to some men...before I became as I am, I once heard an *ereticy*, howling for a mate, a victim. It was enough to make me *almost* follow her to what might've been a worse doom than the one which befell me of my own volition."

Around us, the merciless thump-thump-thump of the bass line from the recording had stopped, as had Ivan, who stood up there, his skin bathed in the same shimmering colors from the monitors as Zivon's had been; yet on Ivan, the effect was clownish, laughable...as was the response to his performance. No ice-filled soda glasses had tinkled in time to his song, and no women were straining their necks to glance at him as he meekly quitted the stage and shuffled back to the table. He refused to look Zivon in the eye as he sat down, and slammed back his remaining Diet Coke. With Lime, and tiny round nubs of nearly-melted ice. Finally, after he drained the glass with a gurgle and a gulp, he said to Zivon, "Was it good? No, wait... was *she* good?"

Zivon waited a beat, then leaned forward toward Ivan and said in a soft, succinct voice, "Absolutely the best, my friend. Thank you for your superb taste in companions." Apparently Zivon was expected to take the stage after any aural disasters like Ivan had "performed," for he got to his feet (and immediately the surrounding crowd stopped talking, and looked expectantly his way, like something out of those old, old TV commercials for that brokerage firm, when everyone would look toward whoever had mentioned the company's name), and began to turn toward the stage, when he paused, then leaned down close to Ivan, and pseudo-whispered just loudly enough for people in South Dakota to hear, too, "And for the record, *you* absolutely *sucked.*"

No one in Mc C's was inclined to disagree with Zivon, based on the susurration of assenting voices and nodding heads which rippled wave-like out from our table.

"You gonna take that?" Ivan huffed, as Zivon took the stage with a wink in his direction, and a nod to me. "Who the fuck does he think he is?"

"Shouldn't that be 'what'?" I asked, as I let the remainder of my soda slide down my throat in a rush of coolness so reminiscent of my tongue-dance with Zivon, I found myself simultaneously shivering and burning at either end.

"What do you mean, 'what'?"

"He's a 'what' not a 'who,' isn't he? Or do you consider vampires to be human now?" I shot back, seconds before the music started up—that old soul classic from Luther Ingram, "If Lovin' You Is Wrong...," not the arrangement from Rod Stewart's remake, or (the gods forbid!) that country-crap remake some big-hair female crooner had shredded—and when Zivon began singing, even Ivan was inclined to keep his mouth shut, for as Zivon sang this time, the entire room grew quiet, down to the shuddering clatter of ice swirling in glasses. And it was not my imagination, not at all, that Zivon was singing directly to *me*, and not to the other deep-breathing, aching women in attendance. *It wasn't him trying to put Ivan down*, I realized. *He meant what he said about me.*

Not that I had any illusions about myself, or my lovemaking abilities...hell, the fact that I'd come here as Ivan's non-date, his ticket to a blood-sucker's cast-offs, was enough to make me realize I wasn't exactly the most desirable, gorgeous female in the Great Plains, let alone the country. Most of the women around me were my equal when it came to looks, while many were far better-looking. But I was a complete loss to understand just what it was about me that he found so worthy, so appealing to his needs.

Unable to find answers within myself, I decided to simply watch Zivon sing, but as my eyes took in his shifting-colors-washed-face, I noticed that his gaze never wavered from my face, my own eyes. From the little Ivan had told me about Zivon's "role" at the club, I understood that following each song, some other lucky meal would be chosen, leaving all those hopefuls sitting in unvented heat, waiting for the next likely temporary mate. It hadn't been that dark in the bar when Zivon and I came back in for me not to have noticed the number of couples sitting two to a chair, or the lap-dances going on along the outer walls.

The smell of sex alone still hung in the air, growing stronger with each syllable Zivon sang, and with each note coming from the speakers, that tension I'd felt when first entering the club less than an hour before continued to build, until it felt like I was barely able to breathe. Only now, I sensed something else—gradually, I could feel other people staring at *me*, some in barely suppressed anger, others in wonderment. And I didn't need to break the anger and wonderment folks into Venus-Mars groups either.

If Zivon came my way once he finished singing, the twice-scorned women would be too furious to seek partners to sate their needs, while the men...who knew what *they'd* do. Watching Zivon, I wondered if he realized my dilemma, and would know what to do...even as I wished he'd do *An Officer and a Gentleman*, and simply scoop me up in his arms, and whisk me out of there. Even though I was pretty damned sure he didn't have a car, or anything else with which to drive me home.

Then...the song was over, and Zivon let go of the microphone, but he didn't relinquish the stage. Not just yet. Our eyes locked, and I was the one who nodded, and smiled to show him it was, indeed, all right with me. More slowly than before, he made his way off the stage, and veered off toward the bar itself, close to the entrance, where a row of pretty young trailer-trash types were sitting on those ubiquitous bar stools that squeak and groan no matter how lightweight the person sitting on them may be. Holding out his arms, he scooped all three women off those noisy plastic perches, and ushered the trio out the door, letting in a swirling blast of snowy air behind them.

For his part, Ivan-the-Shamed slinked away from the table, in search of bypassed booty while I told myself, *It's what he's been doing for centuries. It's the only way he can survive*, as I went to the bar (the three empty stools still bore the ass-impressions of their previous, now other-wise engaged occupants, while the air retained a trace of their knock-off perfumes) to order another drink. Noticing my attempt to put a brave face on my disappointment, the guy behind the bar—I don't know if you could call him a bartender, since all he did was sell cans of soda, but soda jerk implied someone with skills beyond that of opening a cooler door, picking out a can, and pouring the contents over a large glass filled with ice—smiled at me and said over the din of some woman bravely wailing her way though "Rock On, Gold Dust Woman," "First timer, uh? Don't worry, he'll pick you again. No one who hears him can stay away. And all of them's thirsty. And no one who's been out in that parking lot will ever want to hear anyone else sing at *any* karaoke bar. But I have to say it, you're classier than most of what crawls over that threshold. You a native?"

"Was...years ago. Went to high school here, then split when I got my diploma. On the bus before the janitor swept up the auditorium aisles after the ceremony." I gingerly sat down on one of the women's vacated stools (there was still a faint hint of warmth on the vinyl), and added, "I'm just in town for a friend's wedding. But...I'm between jobs, so who knows? I might stay awhile. I can go back to temp work if I have to. Not that I want to...."

"Yeah, my sister's a temp worker, office computer stuff. The other workers resent her because she makes more than they do. But she never stays, 'cause if she's hired on regular—"

"—she's paid less," I finished with a sigh. The man's words made me think about Zivon, the club's "regular" singer, whose pay could never be documented for tax purposes on any available government form—

"You know what he is, don't you?" I leaned close to the man, but all he did was let loose an explosive laugh, before nodding through his laughter-induced tears. "Hell yes, I knowed what he was soon as he first came in here. My family's been here on the plains since there was *nothing* from here to there. Ukrainian on my dad's side, Norwegian on the old lady's. Hell, we knows our vampires. Or *uppyrs*, as Dad' grand-daddy called 'em. That old coot probably knew some of the fellahs who branded ole Loverboy's ribcage for 'im. Zivon, he's been around a looong time. Long as he don't bite necks, make hisself obvious, I don't give a squirt what he does out there. Not like we're living in a sea of virgins, eh? He brings in the butts in the seats, and keeps 'em coming back for more. Plus, the man can sing, if you like someone who 'nunciates like a sissy-ass. At least he's in tune."

Sensing that our conversation was over, I wandered away from the bar, drink in hand, and was mildly surprised to find my table still unoccupied. Up on the stage, the singer swayed like a *faux* Stevie Nicks, flapping the opened sides of her sweaterset cardigan like a stole, trying to make her voice all the more gravel-rough, while at least a few guys were nodding in time with the music, no doubt hoping to score, when two fast-moving wing-like closed pink palms and tight-positioned fingers came up against my face from behind, and covered my eyes and the top of my nose with a steady, smooth warmth. Before I could cry out, I heard a voice murmur from just behind my left ear, "I really did mean what I said, to your companion. I'd *never* lie about that," before the hands pulled away from my face, and Zivon swung around me, and sat himself down in one of the three empty chairs. None of the women from the bar were with him, but I knew from the intense heat of his palms which still lingered on my face that he'd been with all of them. His face was flushed, and even the raised scar on his chest was deep blush pink. Before I could say anything, he took both of my hands in his, holding them firmly but gently in his own thoroughly warmed fingers, and said softly, "I only wanted to be warm while you were too...like equals, if only for a few minutes. So you'd know what I was like, once. Not merely a *taker* of your heat. But a giver," and he suddenly leaned forward and kissed me on the lips, just enough to brush his fevered flesh against mine, before returning to his seat.

I had no idea what to say.

But I didn't pull my hands away from his, so I was able to feel them gradually lose their fresh heat as yet another woman took the stage, this one dressed like an escapee from one of those Goth clubs Zivon had told me about...dark-rimmed eyes, lips so crimson they were less than a shade away from dried-blood-black, and a dress that barely covered her rounded pale A cups, let alone looked like it would stay in one piece if a good stiff breeze hit her, the thing was so fragile and tattered, while her shoes were easily a size too big for her, giving the dark-haired young woman a sort of Tim Burtonesque aura of desperate decay, or impending dissolution. Zivon noticed how I stared at the woman, and turned his head toward her—when he saw her, his fingers curled into talon-like claws, the short nails raking my palms, and he let out a long, moaning breath which ended with a single, barely-mouthed word:

"*Ereticy.*"

No way, I told myself, *Not two vampires in one club, and not out* here*, in the middle of zero-population-growth-ville.*

Beside me, Zivon was saying in a low drone, "I...know...this one. Remember her, from Ukraine. Tasya Mauraska. Same... dress. More worn...can you smell it?

Realizing that he was speaking to me, and not merely to himself anymore, I took a deep breath, and found myself with two lungs filled with something sickly-sweet to the point of foulness, a cloying odor which hinted at things far beyond the hot odor of sex alone.

Beyond and above us, she tapped one foot in time to the

music coming from the speakers, then began singing that old Pat Benatar classic, "Heartbreaker," only hearts weren't broken when she opened her mouth—eardrums were. Now I knew what Zivon meant by "unseemly cries"...and he'd been right when he said that some men wouldn't mind at all—in fact, I noticed more than one man in the club leaning forward, oblivious to the other women around them, straining for more.

I'd never heard anything so raucous, so ear-twistingly loud and strident in my life. Alley cats screwing were melodious in comparison. Yet the men—save for Zivon—were entranced with this harpy, this...thing. Pulling me up to my feet, he draped one arm across my shoulders, and hurried me out of the club, back into the bracing slap of the snow-flecked winds outside. But we stopped next to the door, with Zivon shielding me from the cold with his body, as he said, "I should've known she'd come here...she's probably been to every other bar like this from coast to coast. Feeding, then destroying. Her kind is too leech-like to die...she gives nothing back, just *takes*—"

"How much does she take?" I found myself asking, while wrapping both arms around his waist, under his rough leather jacket. Zivon leaned his head close to mine, so that our foreheads touched, and whispered with coppery-scented breath, "Every last thing. She's not like me...my kind. She *drains*, completely. Then moves on. First she takes their soul, their faith in what is true and real, then...everything else. What's left isn't capable of being a vampire. She leaves *nothing*."

Somehow, knowing that Ivan-the-ever-hopeful was still in that bar, eager for whatever it was he was hoping one of these women could give to him, be it sex, attention, or merely the time of night, I took comfort from Zivon's words. He seemed to sense that, as he held me close and said, "Tasya had to die before she became what she was...but you need not. If...it is what you really want."

Had he absorbed some of my desires along with my blood? Could he have heard me talking in the bar, while he was out in the parking lot, doing whatever it was he needed to do with those three women? Perhaps he was an old enough soul (if vampires retained some vestige of their souls in the after-afterlife) to simply be able to read me without being privy to my thoughts.

"Will it change you? Make you—"

"Alive again? No...but it won't change me, either. We'll be more alike, that is all. You'll need the way I do, and you'll feed as I do, but when you need, I'll need too, and afterward...we can share each other, and what we've taken from those willing to give it. It's not such a bad life, singing for one's supper, as it were. Perhaps, it will make things more equal here, once *she's* gone."

And he's *gone*, I mentally added, knowing all too well that Ivan would beat a path to that...thing on the stage once she shut her dark-ringed mouth and gave up her place between the monitors.

Pulling Zivon even closer to me, close enough for me to feel his chest shuddering against mine, I asked, "How do I do it? Tell me before I come to my senses, or whatever it is mortal women are supposed to do around someone like you—"

"Not here," Zivon said, pulling his arms from around my waist, and motioning for me to follow him. We were moving quickly side by side toward the rear of the building, toward a distant copse of elderly box elders, their spider-web tangle of small upper branches seemingly dusting the lower edges of the moon above. And beyond the elders was a dark-windowed old farmhouse, barely visible from the highway. Zivon and I silently made our way to the house, which—as I could see as we came closer—had a small path shoveled from the front door to the path we walked, so someone still occupied it.

"Not the coffin or hole in the dirt you were expecting, is it?" he asked with a smile, as he opened the aged wood and rust-filigreed screen door, then pushed in the solid oak door beyond. Without saying anything else, he led me into his home, which was dimly lit by the moonlight streaming through the wavy glimmer-glass panes of the house's many windows. As he led me toward a staircase to the rear of the ground floor rooms,

I saw vague furniture shapes, and what looked like kerosene lamps of a vintage design. The stairs were well-worn, and carpet-less, wide enough for us to ascend them side-by-side. The entire upper story was one attic bedroom, dominated by a brass-framed double bed covered with what looked like antique quilts and soft feather pillows. As if able to anticipate my inevitable question, Zivon stood behind me and said as he wrapped his arms around me, pressing my back against his chest, "The native soil I need to sleep on is in a bag, under the bed. I could never get used to sleeping *in* it...too much of a reminder of what I became by accident, not design. So...are *you* sure? Once you do this, you cannot change the process...or so those vampire groupies in Chicago told me. Even as they refused to go through with it themselves."

Despite the chill in the air, I felt the sure heat of certain desire pulse through my entire body, and as I turned around within the tight circle of Zivon's close grasp, I looked up at him and said, "Tell me what to do. *Now*," then kissed him on the chin, the lips, his eyes.

Walking as one being to the bed, Zivon gently sat me down on the edge, then, as he slowly undid my sweater buttons, my jeans zipper, and reverently disrobed me, he whispered in the moon-washed semi-darkness, "This time, you'll have to bite my throat...I show you where...then all you need to do is drink me in, swallow down as much of my blood as you can...you'll know when you've had your fill. Once you've changed, you'll be as I am...what I am, you'll be."

As he pulled away the last of my clothes, I began unbuttoning his shirt, then slid it off his shoulders along with his jacket, where it landed on the floor with a muffled thump, like a felled body at our feet. Unzipping his jeans, I used my thumbs to yank then down around his ankles, and as he leaned over to kick them off his legs, along with his boots, I said softly, my voice echoing in the wide nearly empty confines of the room, "What *we'll* be, together."

In that pale sugary light, Zivon's body was that of a young,

young man, still taut and smooth-skinned, and as he tenderly placed his hands on my shoulders, and laid me down on that soft bed, before climbing on next to me, he said, "And you'll never change, from what you are now...is that enough for you? To do this?"

"As long as you're part of the bargain, yes, absolutely *yes*," I replied, while feeling his neck for his pulse.

Guiding my hand to a spot near the left side of his neck, he whispered, "*Here*. Don't hesitate, *do* it. Bite down hard, press your lips against me, and *drink*. As if I am your lifeblood—"

Up close, his flesh smelled faintly of sweet grasses and things earthy, with a hint of minerals, and I only hesitated for a second before positioning my incisor against his skin, and with a rush of carnal urgency, sank my teeth into his pliant flesh with a soft squelching noise; quickly positioning my lips around the wound, I sucked, and felt—

—an explosion of coldness, tinged with an unexpected sweetness, a blossoming bright taste that was more cinnabar than cinnamon, yet spicy-dulcet, which blossomed on my tongue, and bathed my inner vision with a heady, strobing pulse of pure scarlet, and all I could think was, *Red is supposed to be a hot color, but nothing could be so cold, so incredibly fresh, so unabashedly raw and biting....*

And the harder I drank of him, the closer Zivon held me, wrapping his legs around mine, brushing his erect, frigid manhood against my thighs, my belly, before entering me with a swift, startlingly deep stroke, that served to join us into one continuous being, one which shared not only the same blood, but the same flesh, the same cold inner fire. With each swallow of his essence, I felt that unearthly chill ripple through me like an orgasm, until every cell in my body shivered, then passed into a calm, still wintry peace.

Sensing on the most primitive, innate level that I'd swallowed my fill of him, I broke contact with his flesh with a gentle sucking sound, then probed the wound with my tongue, before kissing it better. Face-to-face in the milky white-blue moonlight, I stared into his eyes, now narrow rings of sapphire and steel, circling two inky pools into which I willingly drowned the last of my remaining humanity.

This time, when he climaxed within me, I felt a burst of gelid moisture burst forth and blossom within the deepest parts of my body, and as he gradually grew flaccid and soft within my muscle-ringed vagina, he whispered, "I cannot make you with child, but what I've give will protect you, from any sicknesses your...nourishment might pass along. You can never die, now. But together, we can live, through others—"

"All I care about is the 'together' part," I murmured, before pulling him closer to me, and drifting off into what passes for sleep in our kind....

* * * * * * *

When Zivon and I stepped into Mc C's the next evening, the man behind the bar gave both of us a knowing look, before waving us over to speak to him. As we approached the bar, arm-in-arm, the guy lifted up my jacket, which I'd left hanging on the back of my chair a lifetime ago, and silently handed it to me, before saying to Zivon, "Now don'tcha go goin' off early on me like that again...I hadda listen to that damn virgin shredder all night, until she finally took off with that Yura doofus. I just hope she don't come back here—bad enough when all the broads are in heat, but handling a buncha guys with—"

Nodding so that the barkeep would shut up, Zivon said, "No, it won't happen like that again. Thanks for saving my lady's coat for her."

"I gots ole Ivan's coat back here too—either one of you gonna be seeing him around, you think?"

If even a fraction of what Zivon had told me about the *ereticy* Tasya was true, I doubted anyone would be seeing much of Ivan Yura anytime soon...at least not needing a coat, unless it served as a shroud. But the man's comment about her being a "virgin shredder" did make me laugh, and instinctively Zivon caught my thought, and began laughing, too, before he and I stepped away from the bar, and mingled with our waiting meals for that night.

That was the first night of our lifeless life together, filled with song, adulation, and that all-too-brief inner flame from beings as insubstantial to us as stick matches. Nightly, Zivon and I take turns at the microphone, making sure we manage to watch each other in the ever-changing glow of the lyrics-covered monitors on stage—and even if the burning warmth of desire which fills me nightly has its origins in men other than Zivon, just as the fire in his flesh derives from blood other than mine, there is always that moment, come closing time, when we bask in the last of that pseudo heat, and consummate our mutual desire in a fleeting resemblance of purely carnal human lust.

In time, we've settled on our own personal signature songs, his being "In Your Eyes," and mine "The First Time Ever I Saw Your Face"—and woe to anyone who dares sing our sigs. After all, once they're kicked out of Mc C's, on our orders, they're on their own—

—and you never know when the next shredder in the next club down the line might be an *eretic*y. From what Zivon told me, those creatures do need to make a lot of noise, and if there's one place where it's socially acceptable now-a-days *to* make infernal racket, it's a karaoke bar....

AFTERWORD

In the film *The Big Lebowski*, a rather clueless bowler named Donnie (played to needy, nerdy perfection by the sublime Steve Buscemi) keeps butting into conversations about which he has but the barest understanding, making *non sequiturs*, until another bowler named Walter (John Goodman) barks back at him, "Donnie, you're out of your element!" Well, when it comes to understanding the behaviors of the characters in this story, *I* was the one clearly out of my element.

First off, understand that I am perhaps one of the most boring human beings on the planet. Like Chris-Ware-graphic-novel-protagonist *blah*. Don't smoke, drink or do drugs. Don't twitter, or blog. Don't even wear make-up (at least not for the last 15 + years). Live with my cats. Can't drive. Haven't even gone bowling, for cryin' out loud. Never dated, ever. And I certainly haven't been in a karaoke bar, either.

But...a long (I mean *long*) time pen-pal of mine, John Postovit, is one of those folks who lives for new experiences, love to travel, has multiple degrees, has worked many diverse jobs, ridden an elephant, visited bars in Bulgaria where the barkeeps set the bar top on fire, and has accomplished far more than yours truly ever will, despite being a few years younger than I am. Writes wonderful letters, often detailing his travels and various other cultural experiences. He was the one who called a Fargo bar the "Sodom and Gomorrah of the High Plains" and he lived in Fargo for many years. He *has* been to karaoke bars, and wrote to me about his experiences once a few years ago...right around the time I got an invite to submit a story to a hetero-story-only vampire erotica anthology. Now I'd been sick for a couple of months with back-to-back (but different) cases of the flue prior to getting the invite, so, since the deadline was close, and I really didn't have many ideas, I cobbled together this little tale (ok, not so little, it's 7k long). While I've never been to North Dakota (the closest I've been is the Twin Cities area), John has described the place frequently enough, plus sent a few picture from time to time, for me to get a rough feel of the place. Plus I've seen the Coen's *Fargo* like about at least a dozen times, so...I tried my hand at a Great Plains vampire story.

This one didn't sell, although editors have found nice things to say about it in general when I occasionally drop it in the mail with a SASE. I sorta like it; much of the slang comes from a book on various slang terms associated with all sorts of social and sports subgroups, which I've often used in my work mainly because I *am* out of my damn element about 90% of the time. Sometimes it works. This time, it didn't quite work, but I still like some of the passages in here. At any rate, it's the last vampire story I've written to date—maybe I might write another in the future, but don't hold your breath or sharpen your fangs in anticipation. I think my vampire-story-muse has left the building, along with Elvis. But I thought someone might still enjoy it, so here it is....

And, of course, when I wrote this, I had no idea that I'm actually part Russian....

DARK LADONNA

Just as I was about to unhook my bra, Kenneth rapped light-ly on the dressing-room door, prior to nudging it open wide enough for him to snake his right hand and forearm through. He was clutching a pink plastic bottle of baby oil, the kind with a flip-hinge cap, in his maggot-squishy fingers.

"Be a dear, would, and smear this on before the sitting, espe-cially...down *there*...." Kenneth's voice trailed off to an embar-rassed mumble.

Considering that he'd seen me naked for two to three hours a day, five days a week, that Kenneth still felt the need to rely on euphemisms like "down *there*" for the more accurate mons, or mound of Venus, or outer labia, or even the ultra-scholarly pudendum, never failed to amuse me. Unpeeling his moist fingers from the small pink bottle, I replied, "Will do...gimme a couple of minutes, ok?" Kenneth let out another mortified grunt of what I assumed was assent before withdrawing his hand and closing the dressing room door.

Once I'd undone my bra, and kicked off my panties, I began squirting the oil on my limbs and torso, before rubbing the clear, slightly greasy emollient across my lightly-tanned flesh. (Usually, I wasn't a sun-baby, but when Kenneth hired me for this particular sitting, he insisted that I pay a weekly visit to the tanning salon, with him footing the bill, by using the excuse that "Pale just won't do for this painting...and while you're at it, could you go back to your natural hair color? Blonde isn't what I'm looking for this time, either....") The dressing room had one of those on-wall electric fan-type heaters, and the combination of the warm, slightly undulating blasts of air from the heater and the fine coating of oil on my exposed skin felt so sensuous, I was almost tempted to tell Kenneth that it would take me a little longer to get ready than usual...but, remembering how well he paid me for each sitting (far more than my usual art class modeling fees—and I only had him painting me, not a room full of gawking art education students), I decided not to keep him waiting.

Especially since this was the last sitting for this painting.

Before I flipped the bottle's hinged cap back into place, I did aim the opening "down *there*" and squeezed out an extra dribble of oil, which I allowed to slowly ooze down over my mons and across my outer and inner labia. Using the first three fingers of my free hand, I gently massaged the oil over and into each pucker and wrinkle of flesh, avoiding my clit least I get too involved in the job prior to the sitting. After all, Kenneth had me posed with my arms above waist-level....

Despite the fact that I'd been posing for this latest painting of Kenneth's for over a month, my heart never failed to pound just a little harder, while my breath caught in my throat for an almost panicky second, whenever I saw the sitting area. Between the time when I'd come in for the sitting and scurry off to remove my clothes, and the time (usually no more than five minutes later) when I'd step out again, *sans* clothes, Kenneth would somehow change a normal, well-lit artist's studio into what had to be at least the second or third ring of Hell...or a place far less hospitable.

Save for a diffuse cone of light near his easel, the room would be bathed in carmine and ocher, the gels used to tint the lights doubled in their holders, until only the murkiest hues shone through, and everything that could be sat or reclined upon was draped in black and magenta velveteen and wedding-gown-heavy satin, even the section of floor in front of the sitting area. Here and there, thick blue-black, purple and dried-blood-red candles flickered, their flames somehow lower and...redder than usual.

Oh, I *knew* that Kenneth was no magician, no alchemist; he simply kept drop cloths over the velveteen and satin drapes, just to keep them dust-and-lint-free, and if a person uses a lighter, lighting over a dozen candles takes what, a minute or less? A mere flick of a switch accounted for the ruddy lighting—

But the knowing did little to stop the pounding of my heart, or the involuntary catch in my breath; I suppose it was simply the type of scene that would give anyone pause...especially if that "anyone" had to sit in the middle of all that enveloping blood-dark murkiness for two or three unmoving hours, with only the liquid *splots* of Kenneth squeezing out fresh blobs of paint for company.

"Oh, you look perfect! And you've even started to let your hair grow out there...the stubble looks like tiny thorns...perfect, perfect," Kenneth muttered, while busying himself with coaxing fresh blops of paint out of the small aluminum tubes; looking down at my mons (usually shaved bare for swimming and gymnastics, but I'd finished with both sports at the end of the season), I saw that he was right—the rounded cleft mound was studded with hundreds of short, even bristles of oiled black hair. Somehow, my own mons looked strange to me, as if it wasn't mine, but someone else's...someone more like the red-fleshed woman in Kenneth's painting, the woman I'd never quite thought of as *me* before.

Unlike some artists (or just plain art teachers, like Kenneth), who religiously guard their work in progress against prying eyes, Kenneth let me see what he'd done after each after-noon-into-evening once the sitting was over. While I'd seen a few of his earlier works (and even posed for a couple of them) in the yearly faculty art shows, none of them came close to what he was accomplishing this time around. His earlier stuff was...basically ok, nothing to make a person think, Hey, this guy should be doing more than teaching. But this painting, this "Dark Ladonna," was another matter entirely....

Despite a lack of the usual black-magic/Satanic/otherworldly props like inverted crosses, or horned whatsits, or pentagrams, there was no mistaking what the woman and black-swathed child in the thickly paint-daubed canvas were supposed to represent. An unholy Madonna and Child, although Kenneth confided in me that "that singer simply ruined the original name...at least 'Ladonna' still means 'the lady'...." But once a person looked long enough at that oil-paint-layered canvas, with its unexpected peaks and broad, sweeping arcs of flatly-laid-on pigments, it was clear that *this* Mother and Child pre-dated any known language, religion or culture. She and her bulky-swaddled offspring were primordial, perhaps hewn from the moist flesh of the earth itself.

The head of the woman (my head, I now realized, with a genuine ripple of shock and astonishment that ran through my body, only to culminate in a twinge of pleasure-pain centering around my clitoris) was lolling back, to rest against a black ill-defined shape rising out of the red-ebony haze around her, while her arms were loosely draped on other dark mound-like protrusions surrounding her. Near the left hand, a black-bundled baby (only the pale crescent of a hairless forehead and one oddly-curled hand could be seen; Kenneth had painted the child—an old plastic baby-sized doll—early on, during the first week, and I never saw it again during the remainder of the sitting) rested on a swell of carmine, as if hovering above a pool of its mother's birthing blood. The mother wasn't touching the child; it was obvious from her/my expression that she was more than ready to start the whole gestation process anew.

For the legs of the woman were brazenly open, the thighs positioned well apart, to reveal the deep gape of her vagina...if the woman in the painting had had a set of female organs, that is. At the time, as I prepared for the last sitting, Kenneth had left that part of the woman uncompleted; while the rest of her was red-defined with thick daubs and swaths of oil-paint, complete with reddish highlights on her body and flowing black hair, there was only a thin layer of base-coat in the spot where her legs joined her body, nothing more. Aside from the mons, labia and vaginal opening, the painting had seemed to be complete yesterday....

Behind his easel, Kenneth was done preparing his palate; setting down the paint-laden free-form piece of wood on the small table next to his easel—which was, I now noticed, positioned much closer to the sitting area than usual—he softly clapped his pudgy hands and said, "Anytime you're ready...I hope you don't mind my coming in a little closer...it's the...uhm, most important part of the painting and all...," until his voice trailed off apologetically.

If any other painter I'd posed for would have moved in a little closer so as to better look at my exposed genitals, I would've minded, and plenty (art education majors aren't the only ones who gawk), but Kenneth was Kenneth, and that made all the difference. Not that he was gay; Momma's boy was more like it. The kind of guy who lives with his mom long after he either wants to or has to, simply because he's used to it, and hasn't the nerve to try something different. The kind of man whose white-bread-in-the-dotted-wrapper looks (pasty face, love-handles jutting out above his corduroy slacks, terminally middle-aged, thinning hair, *et al.*) brand him for what he is—Mr. Boredom. With tenure.

But since this was Kenneth, I just smiled, and padded over to the draped riser where I'd reclined for the last thirty days or so, before positioning myself before him. This time, though, I was slightly reluctant to open my legs and drape them across the adjacent risers; while Kenneth probably knew every wrinkle and pucker of my labia better than my gynecologist did, that he was specifically staring at me *there*, while capturing those same wrinkles and puckers on his already paint-loaded canvas, made me feel squeamish for probably the first time since I'd started modeling on the side. Every other time, just my *body*, in all its non-organ-specific-glory, had been on display. Not the center of *me*.

And not for everyone who later viewed the painting to see—

"Uhm, Kenneth, is this one going to be part of the next

faculty show?" I asked, while positioning my arms and head; with my head slightly back, my features were a bit distorted in the painting (as I'd seen so far), but sudden images of all my professors, all my fellow students, staring at my softly gaping vagina, crept into my mind, and refused to leave.

"Actually, no...I'm going to have a gallery showing, in a real art gallery, in a couple of months. A few of my old pieces will be shown too, but *very* few. This is going to be my coming-out as a real artist...not a faculty art-fart," he said, with a real smile in his voice. The warmth in his voice wasn't sexual, just friendly; I was finally able to relax, as I let the muscles in my thighs and lower abdomen go loose and easy, so that I all but melted across the fuzzy-silky draped risers.

The air around us was warm from the flickering candles, an uneven, varying warmth that caressed my slippery flesh like tiny puffs of air from the nostrils of someone who is very close to one's body. And the arc lights cast a more even warmth, one that pressed down on my bare flesh like dozens of over-lapping palms, so I found myself beginning to sweat, the drop-lets of moisture mingling with the oleaginous sheen which was already reflecting the surrounding lights in flame-like overlap-ping pools of henna and crimson, until the runnels of sweat created branching patterns in that swirl of hot color covering my body.

Glancing down, past my jutting, pucker-nippled breasts, and the slight doubled-over swell of my belly, I was mesmerized by the nap-like effect of my growing-in public hair over my red-lit mound of Venus, the hairs forming a parted-wave pattern over each cleft half of that mound of swollen flesh. Again, I was struck by the feeling that this body was not quite mine, but instead something formed by globs of paint, something that—once dried on the canvas—would no longer be a part of me at all, but something alien, something...malign.

After all, *this* Ladonna wasn't cradling her child in her arms.

Across the narrow space between Kenneth and where I reclined in open-legged splendor, I could only see half of his head above the propped-up rectangle of canvas, but the silence in the studio was so complete I could actually hear him smearing the paint on the canvas, a soft, liquid *'plash* that was so sensuous, so...intimate, that I soon felt yet another dribble of moisture emerge from my body, "down *there*" as Kenneth would have so prissily dubbed it. Each time his head bobbed down, I heard another silky stroke of his brush against the grainy canvas, and soon my labia was twitching in time with the pigments he added to his painting. With each new brush stroke, another set of my muscles seemed to melt within me, so by the time Kenneth paused to uncap another tube of paint, I felt (and must have looked) like a pool of blood, my body all but soaking into the surrounding draped risers....

Closing my eyes, I let lazy, playful thought flit across my mind; memories of boyfriends old and new, the phantom touch of hands on my breasts, my buttocks, the moist softness of tongues on my—

When I felt the first delicate, almost tentative prodding against my outer set of labial lips, I jerked into full, angry consciousness, thinking, Kenneth, you puke, you had to wait until the last damn sitting—until I saw his thinning head of hair bobbing up and down behind the canvas, accompanied only by the random moist *'plash* of the paint-laden brush caressing the canvas. A better look his way revealed his tassel-moccasins crossed primly under his chair, so he wasn't even playing footsies.

You're just horny, I told myself. It's too damn hot, too damn close in here...and you're smeared from forehead to feet with baby oil. Do you honestly think Kenneth would diddle you on the sly?

But, even as I had to answer my own questions with an emphatic No *way*—the gentle prodding became a teasing caress, as...whatever it was massaged and rubbed against my inner labia, then my clit, moving in its own urgent, yet exquisitely slow rhythm, until my thigh muscles jerked involuntarily in time with that unseen fondling, and my pelvis began to thrust up and down, the movement slight but ever so insistent...so *eager.*

And the worst-yet-best-part was, I couldn't quite tell what was teasing and gently kneading my slippery twitching flesh; it was thin and pointed, yet moist, simultaneously finger-tongue-penis-like, but far more flexible and pliant than any of the three normal male appendages...and, perhaps the most erotic thing about it, it was deliciously cool against my tense, fiery flesh, and everywhere it lingered before moving on in a smooth, gliding motion, I felt a protracted sensation of that same tingly coolness, which dissipated with exquisite slowness before the fire once again consumed my flesh, while that thin wand-like pressure move down to other parts of my anatomy, stopping for a moment near the base of my vagina, dipping deep into the well of wetness, then moving to my outer labia, to lazily circle the stiff-haired mons surrounding the inner softness, before it returned to my clitoris, to create a bull's-eye of *cool* around the now-burning flesh, and during all of this, I felt my nipples pucker to the point of painfulness, while my hands grabbed silky bunches of fabric, the fingers curling into claws of trembling flesh-covered bone.

And the lone sound was that of the brush gliding on more paint, that moist, irregular noise which so closely resembled that of someone lapping at my exposed, sweat-and-oil-and-vaginal-juices slick labia but this time, I felt no soft puffs of breath against my skin, only that steady, invasive, sweetly painful probing of...whatever it was that was slowly and methodically driving me to the brink of orgasm.

Then, when I could stand that teasing, circling motion no longer, it briefly stopped, leaving me to gasp and wonder about the reality of what I'd just felt (surely, nothing of or not of this world could ever feel that good, *that* purely sensual)—then, without pause or hesitation, it *entered* me—thrusting hard, fast and deep in my vagina, just a long, thin flexible *sensation* which plowed into my body with a speed and a directness beyond anything I'd previously experienced, and all I could do was continue to flatten myself against the riser, yielding fully to this unseen, but oh so definitely felt invasion of my innermost self, while the tip of the thing brushed up against my cervix, having gone deeper within me than any man's penis, or any vibrator wielded by my own hand, had gone before.

By then, I felt the first twinges of real pain, the kind of pain that negates pleasure, but there was no way to dislodge what was within me, none at all...there were no thighs resting on my own to thrust away, no body at all to slap or punch or shove off of me. Just that deep-probing sensation, thrusting ever-further into my body, beyond what was *meant* to be fucked—

And during all of this, I said nothing, save for letting a few sot moans escape my oil-sheened lips. And Kenneth seemed to notice nothing; his head still bobbed up and down behind that canvas, as if he were sweetly oblivious to what was happening to me...just a balding, plump former art-fart diddling away at his latest canvas, while I was being impaled by something I could only feel....

Then, with a rush of unexpected warmth, of gushing gelid *fullness*, it climaxed within me. For a second, all I could think of was ice, melting fast and slippery on a griddle; the juxtaposition of coolness and intense, spurting warmth made my heart flop furiously beneath my left breast, until that tight-nippled mound of flesh jerked in time with my heartbeats...and then, as unexpectedly as it had come to me, the sensation, the...fullness of it left me.

And, despite the pain it had caused me, I still longed for it to return to me...even as Kenneth clapped those soft-palmed hands of his, and said, "Time to get up now...it's finally done."

Ignoring the dull residual ache in my lower abdomen, I got up to my feet (my body was covered with the powdery black fuzz from the velveteen along my lower legs and buttocks, forming a match to my dripping, black-bristled mons), smiling for Kenneth as I padded around to the front of the canvas...but that smile turned icy and brittle, so fragile I could barely keep it on my face, as I stared at the completed "Dark Ladonna."

That the paint was still wet had to account for some of the

shine and shimmer of the woman's (*my*) gaping, slightly blurred red-tinged genitals, but I doubted that the painting would shine less once it dried.

How he did it, I didn't know, but Kenneth had captured a woman in *heat*, a woman panting and aching and arcing her pelvis forward to get it, and get it *now*. The open wanting and passionless need he'd captured went beyond a mere painted representation of my genitals...he'd dipped his brush into my own psyche, and left it to slowly dry on that canvas. This woman had no need for the child she'd given birth to; she was the Bitch incarnate, nothing but a vessel for sperm, with no sense of shame, no desire to reciprocate her partner's pleasure...just a deep, gaping hole, surrounded by a body. And to see that body look so much like my own was almost (not quite, but damn near almost) enough to make forget the ache and slimy moistness within me, or forget the sense of delicious-but-depraved abandon I'd felt as I'd been diddled, then so rudely entered minutes earlier. In the last hours I'd posed for this painting—the hours in which I'd been violated in the most insidious, yet subtle way—I'd somehow *become* it... while an outwardly dispassionate white-bread Momma's boy methodically got down every runnel of vaginal juice, every captured-in-mid-spasmodic jerk of hot-cold flesh, with just his damned *head* bobbing up and down as he worked.

And, staring at what he'd accomplished, I suddenly felt... worse than cold, virtually detached from my own rage at what had happened/not-quite-happened to me, there in that studio lit in the colors of blood and opened bodies—despite the flicker of the fat dark candles, and the residual warmth of my body radiating from the cloth-draped risers. Even as the center-most source of that preternatural chill continued to worm its way through my lower body, that sensation didn't horrify me as much as the intangible lack of violent anger I now felt; everything sane and logical in my mind screamed at me to feel *something*, to berate Kenneth, to claw at the spreading zone of coolness within me with naked fingers...*something, anything.* Women who'd been pawed on a date worked up far more rage than I could feel after what had happened on those risers, yet, when Kenneth turned his beaming dough-boy face my way, his eyes glittering with expectation tinged with curiosity, I found myself telling him that he'd really done it, created a true masterpiece before feigning the need to use the bathroom, and fleeing for the dressing-room, running on legs gone near-numb with that same dispassionate, near-deadened spreading *nothingness* I felt growing at the core of me.

But even after I'd toweled off the remaining oil and velvet-lint from my flesh (eschewing the chance to douche out that residual creeping chill from my vagina, even though I had the spare pre-filled bottle in my purse—perhaps it was too soon to endure the sensation of being entered by an unyielding presence, perhaps it was...an indefinable *curiosity* about how long the sensation within me would endure on its own), and put on my clothes, I still felt as if my skin was caressed by many frigid hands. The coldness didn't leave me even after I'd re-entered the studio, now white-lit and somehow as sexless and as sterile as Kenneth, who was busy washing off the brush in his jar of mineral spirits, until the cream-colored paint turned the sharp-smelling contents of the jar an opaque, milky white.

As I waited (still becalmed by that ever-growing emotional paralysis) for him to get my sitting fee out of his wallet, something about that squat jar of swirling, slightly oily cream-pigmented liquid began to bother me in an abstract, free-floating sense... until I glanced over at the finished canvas, and felt vague unease turn to a brief stab of icy fear; a fear all the more appalling for its *brevity*. As if, once my mind had time to acknowledge it, it could almost be safely cast aside, as if in anticipation of more important matters with which to occupy my thoughts.

Kenneth had used no cream-tone paint on the canvas that evening.

But, as he extracted the small sheaf of bills from his wrinkled tan wallet, I didn't' dare tell Kenneth what I'd observed, much less what I'd...experienced, least he think me crazy, and least he not hire me again should I ever need money so desperately that I'd willingly face another session posing for him. Even as one part of me began to inwardly chafe from the burrowing, *growing* coldness within (and as yet another, more primitive part of me, a deep-hidden part not quite *yet* soothed-to-calm-ness, let out one last scream of horror at my recent violation, before that scream died down to a *shush*), I took his money with another smile my lips couldn't feel—and told him again what an incredible job he'd done.

Judging by the sudden, broad smile on his face, some-thing told me that Kenneth not only believed my words, but... *somehow*, that he'd anticipated them.

Almost as if he'd *painted* those words in my mind before I'd said them.

* * * * * * *

Kenneth's gallery show came, but it didn't leave the gallery, even after most of the paintings of his—all of them inspired by the same quasi-pagan/religious themes—were bought and removed from the galley, save for "The Dark Ladonna" which wasn't for sale, or so he burbled on the phone to me a few months later, when he called me to find out whether or not I'd be interested in posing for a companion piece to that *other* painting, something Kenneth dubbed "a fertility-type symbol, with heavy erotic overtones...lot of belly and breasts, and little else. Just huge, but still sexy, like a combination of a centerfold and those awful faceless stone fertility figurines form ages ago, the kind cavemen worshipped...that sound like something you'd like to pose for?" As usual, his voice trailed off in apology, even as I detected (from within my numbing cocoon of near-benign apathy) just the slightest hint of malign confidence. As if he did know, somehow, without my needing (or being *able*, for how could I give voice to the unspeakable when I lacked the inner energy to so much as whisper my story to others?) to tell him that—despite being on the Pill—I was already four months pregnant, if that's what I truly was....

I'd seen no doctor, told no one what had happened...for even as I continually denied the possibility (a step which, by its own duration, took me past the time limit of a first-trimester abortion—that time when what is aborted never does look too human anyhow—and any possibility of avoiding questions I knew I could not answer), I kept remembering that jar of mineral spirits, opaquely-stained with that cream-colored paint which never touched the canvas that evening. And with the remembering came the questions...the latest of which was inspired by Kenneth's own off-hand words about cavemen who worshiped fat little stone goddesses—

—how do white-bread Momma's boys worship *their* unholy goddesses? Do they genuflect, or offer sacrifices of sacred pigments?

So, as I forced lips which were bitten bloody from frequent pain-seeking bites—inflicted in the hope of rekindling my lost pain, my paint-pilfered sense of rage—to ask Kenneth when he'd want me to come by his studio, I found myself asking another question...just *how* huge I'd be once this new painting was completed by Kenneth—

—and never mind the oft-asked inner question about *what* was making my lower belly so swollen already, this early in my term...if, indeed, what was happening to me was a pregnancy at all, or a human one *if* it was....

Whatever is happening to me, I have a queasy-yet-calm feeling that Kenneth (thanks to whatever dark gods he's called upon before, when creating "The Dark Ladonna") will capture it *more* than perfectly on canvas, just as he'd somehow managed to capture my former lust, my now-lost passion...but since he's already robbed me of my heat, my fiery rage, I cannot begin to guess what he's planning to take prisoner with his pigments five months from now. Perhaps (I hope against hope), since he's offered up my sexual energies once before, this time he'll restore them to me, in exchange for something else I might not miss so dearly, and need so desperately.

Perhaps, once my time comes due, I might have an answer—

or even my former, active, *living* rage—but no matter what Kenneth's gods ask of him, I'm bound to him with shackles of creamy paint and chains of emotional lethargy.

But I do know, with that calm, cold surety these four long months, that whatever happens, it *will* be a masterpiece...of *some* dark sort.

Kenneth seems *more* than confident of that, as if filled with a certainty which comes from having done what is expected of one, before being granted what one desires.

And for a mere college art professor with tenure, he *has* come a long, long way in the art world. And in a mere four months.

Given that—and given my own unasked-for, albeit-paid-for contribution to the achievement of Kenneth's goals—until the last sitting, I need share in his confidence...either that, or allow the insanity of what has happened to me to forever capture my mind along with my body, with no hope of reclaiming what was once mine to savor. And Kenneth did promise that despite the references (off-hand, I pray) to women of cold, hard stone...so, there might be a chance that *this* time, the probing brush laden with that creamy paint might be warm, and limber, rather than simply cold and stiffly erect.

This time, maybe Kenneth's unknown pigment-gods might be hot, and caress me with unseen fiery fingers, forever dispelling this cool, clinging, *passionless* inner and outer hold on me, and once again releasing my own fire, my own euphoric lusting rage....

The God of *most* men promises to both take away and give to those who believe...but I can only wait in numb anticipation to learn what the gods of white-bred-boys have to offer.

Whatever Kenneth's religion may be, he *did* make me its Ladonna....

AFTERWORD

Personally, I'm torn when trying to write about this one; as far as the story itself goes, I think it turned out fairly well, even though it is a bit on the verbose side, but as far as the creation of this goes, it was an awful process...back in the early 1990s, I'd been in an anthology of semi-erotic horror, and was invited to submit something for a follow-up volume. I ended up sending in three versions of this, all written to the specific orders/requests of the editor, only to find out when I sent in the final draft that the anthology in question had actually been closed to submissions, as in filled and ready to publish, for a few *months*. Naturally, I wasn't too happy about having been goaded into multiple rewrites for something which wasn't going to be even considered for purchase—and that's about all I'll say for now about *that*. But I was *not* happy[1] about it.

It took me a while to find a home for this, but eventually the editor of the late-but-memorable horror zine *Night Terrors*, D. E. Davidson, took it for an e-zine called *Crimson* which he was putting out as a sideline zine. It did well there, earning an Honorable Mention in *YBF&H* that year.

I consider this a gateway story—if I hadn't written it, I might not have written my later erotica stories. I was sort of easing into hard core erotica at the time, and this story is something of a bridge between my darker/edgy horror and my flat-out erotic horror/sf.

---

1. Want a short list of how I felt? Pissed, furious, humiliated, duped, toyed-with, ashamed, and *deeply* miffed. For starters....

AT FUNLAND BY THE
SWINGS, WITH BIG CHUCK

By the end of the first week in August, the kids who visited Funland confided in Big Chuck the Monitor that that new
girl who sat alone next to the swings—not on one of the rust-
chained swings, but on the blunt grass next to the swings—was
really weird.

"She don't know 'bout cooties, Big Chuck. We wiped them
all on her and she just kept 'em."

"I asked her if she saw *The Monkees* last night and she said
she didn't think the zoo was open then—what she mean?"

"Where's she come from? She never says 'cool' or 'guy' or
anything right."

By noon, fifteen of the neighborhood regulars had come
to Big Chuck, the college kid who helped watch over the tiny
children's amusement park each summer, with their tales of
how different that "funny-looking" girl was. How she didn't
know about *The Dating Game*, or read Nancy Drew books, or
remember what night *Star Trek* was on, even play tether ball.

The first couple of days she'd wandered into Funland, with
its small assortment of scaled-down "kiddie" rides, snack
booths and simple bottle toss and basketball throw games, no
one had paid much attention to her, but by now the other kids
had glommed to the fact that she wasn't just a stranger in their
neighborhood...she was strange, period.

But Big Chuck—so dubbed by the elementary-school-age
children he looked after during the day because he was over six

feet tall, and called by the same name by his college-age female contemporaries for a somewhat different reason—had noticed that the new little girl was odd long before the rest of the kids caught on.

It was the way she just sat, not running around spreading cooties, or giggling over by the ice cream stand, or just twisting her long dishwater blonde hair around her fingers, the way the other girls passed the time. But she wasn't cowed-quiet, like some of the browbeaten kids who hung around Funland during the three months it was open each summer, before the real amusement parks and carnivals had long since passed through town, on the way to bigger venues to the south.

This quiet kid was simply content to sit there by the swings, taking things in. As if this was all new to her; the used-car-lot style flag-like banners stringing the booths together, the sweetish-sickly aroma of cotton candy and slushy cones, the needs-oiling squeal of the go-carts in their pen. No parents ever brought her to Funland; Big Chuck noticed that by the second day. He liked that. Parents who cut loose the apron strings got his vote. Best way; open the front door and let 'em go.

Not that the streets were a good place for kids to roam, but that was why the Town Council had set up Funland in one of the town parks, close to the year-round set-up of swings and slides. The kids could vent their energies in Funland, and their parents didn't have to worry, because Big Chuck, who came well-recommended by his *alma mater*, was there, ready in case of any emergency. And he didn't breathe down their necks...let their teachers do that come fall.

In this park-like place, surrounded by and dotted with trees and bushes beyond the booths, as well as that set-up of swings, tire-jungle, monkey bars—funny, she didn't know about *The Monkees*—and tether-ball poles, the kids were safe as long as Big Chuck was around. Nice, clean-cut, gangly Big Chuck, with a supply of Band-Aids, Bactine, and Vicks Cough Drops in his slacks pockets. (No hippie bell-bottoms on Big Chuck; come graduation he was headed for the Peace Corps.) Big Chuck had a supply of quarters in his back pocket, too.

But Big Chuck didn't dispense his quarters the same way he did the Band-Aids, Bactine or cough drops, by giving them out for "owies" and coughs. The kids at Funland had to earn a quarter from Big Chuck, and even if a kid did get one, he or she could never tell where he or she got it. That was part of the Big Secret between Big Chuck and them. A Funland secret.

Only some of the neighborhood kids received those shiny new quarters from Big Chuck. Not the ones whose parents brought them to Funland, and picked them up an hour later. And never the gabby ones whose teachers would pin long black construction paper "Tattle Tails" on their sweaters come fall. Big Chuck wasn't just a nice guy, he was a smart guy. He picked only the quiet, nice little boys and girls for his special quarters. And they didn't have to do a lot to earn those shiny silver coins. But the kids who got the money from Big Chuck did wonder why their parents never paid them a quarter for taking off their underpants at home, but none of them asked their Mommies and Daddies about it. That would've meant breaking the big Funland secret, and then Big Chuck wouldn't give them any more coins, for good stuff like orange Push-Ups from the ice cream stand, or for an extra ride on the merry-go-round.

(Sometimes Big Chuck did strange things to them that tickled, but they never giggled, just in case Big Chuck got mad and forgot to give them a quarter when he was done.)

And Big Chuck had begun to pay attention to the new little girl with the big head and the tiny, baby-like hands right away; as he watched her from his favorite spot close to the big tree near the go-cart pen, his fingers rubbed and rubbed the quarters in his left back pocket. For the past few weeks, he'd paid out money, an awful lot of it, to most the kids playing here today. He knew them better than their folks did, better even than their doctors.

"Familiarity breeds contempt," or so said one of his profs at the university. Big Chuck had a better saying, Familiarity breeds boredom, he told himself, as the coin between his thumb and forefinger grew greasy from being rotated so much.

He always like the quiet kids, but this one was special. For one thing, she didn't wear shorts, or pedal pushers, or jeans, but had on one of those short-skirted sun dresses, the kind that rides up to the thighs and above when a little girl sits cross-legged on the ground. Like the girl was doing now. The kind of dress which shows a small white rectangle of exposed panty, peeking from between small open legs.

Big Chuck's fingers stopped rubbing the coin. She was looking at him. The sun-warmed skin under his crew-cut began to tingle. She was smiling, a sunny little smile which showed off a full set of even, tiny teeth. Big Chuck wondered what tiny baby teeth like that felt like.

Now she was patting the ground next to her, on the side away from the rust-mottled swings. The side close to the tall bushes. Opening a small plastic purse, she extracted a yellow pocket comb, which she ran through her long straight dirty-blonde hair. The kind of blonde Big Chuck saw on the college girls all the time, blonde-growing-into-light-brown. Big Chuck jerked as he heard the decisive click as she snapped the purse shut after replacing the comb.

Putting down the purse—in the past six days she'd been coming to Funland, she'd always had that cheap all-plastic purse close at hand—she picked up an empty eight-ounce 7-Up bottle, and began to blow across the top of it, creating a low, moaning drone.

She didn't take her eyes off him; wise eyes locked on his. Rubbing the coin frantically between the slippery-hot fingers, Big Chuck ambled over to the little girl by the swings, a big smile creasing his tanned face. Those kids who saw him go up to the girl knew enough to play somewhere else. They understood the unspoken rules of the Big Funland Secret Game. No peeking, for one thing. And no making trouble while Big Chuck and his friend were busy elsewhere. Just so none of the grown-ups would start asking why Big Chuck wasn't keeping order, like he was hired to do. Soon, the other children were on the rides, or standing by the candy booth.

"Hi." Big Chuck hunkered down in front of the girl, knees spread out wide. She smiled shyly in return, before blowing across the top of the bottle again.

"That fun?"

A nod of her big head.

"Can I try it?"

A coy shake of her head, followed by a bigger smile.

Big Chuck like that in a kid. Not big-mouthed, but fey all the same. Nice bare legs, with gently-swelling calves which met white ankle socks. And that tiny, short skirt. Like something out of that book he'd read in Modern Novels 355. Lolita.

"OK...can you talk?" Big Chuck crinkled his eyes, against the descending sun behind the girl.

This time, she laughed. "Sure," she said in a surprisingly husky but small voice. "'bout what?" She rested the bottle on the scruffy grass, but didn't let go of it.

Big Chuck sat down cross-legged in front of her, saying "Some of those kids been giving you a hard time?"

"I dunno," she shrugged, her eyes downcast, even as a smile played on her pale lips.

"Yeah, they can be mean, when they don't understand. Just because you're not into passing cooties, or watching *The Monkees*, they peg you for being weird...but I don't think you're weird at all."

"No?" An abrupt tilt of her head, as she looped her hand through the strap of her purse.

"Why should I think you are? Guy, I think you're a nice kid. And I like your dress." He looked down at her skirt, and below. Suddenly, the girl straightened one leg, to scratch an itch on her tanned knee (the golden sunlight made the fine hairs on her skin gleam), and her panties moved aside ever so slightly. But enough.

She kept smiling at him.

"What's your name?" Big Chuck asked, his eyes not focused on her face.

"'manda," she said coyly, not moving her leg.

"That's nice," Big Chuck mumbled, staring, before saying, "I know a rhyme...."

Big Chuck waited until she looked quizzically at him, before solemnly chatting, "I see Paris, I see France, I see—a little girl's underpants!"

Giggling, she asked, "Know any more?" and didn't re-cross her legs.

"Nope...sorry. Hey, know what? All time you've been coming to Funland, I've never seen you buy yourself an ice-cream bar, or go on any of the rides." Big Chuck paused, eyes downcast, before asking gently, "Haven't you got any money?"

"Uh-uh," she said, not seemingly perturbed, then picked up the bottle and began to tootle across the top of it, a mournful hoot.

"Wouldn't you like some? Wanna know where to earn some?"

Her pale eyes blank, she shrugged, then said, "Yeah," as if having the money to take in the attractions at Funland wasn't a very big deal.

'You don't have to spend the money here," Big Chuck added, placing his hand in his pocket full of quarters, filling the warm air with a delicate tinkling sound, one which the other kids knew very well.

She cocked her head slightly at the sound.

"Know what this is, 'manda?"

"Change?" Something about her *blasé* tone niggled the back of his mind, but Big Chuck was too excited to dwell on it.

"Yeah...change...quarters. Guess who for?"

"I dunno," but her eyes did know.

Big Chuck smiled down at her, and her soft brownish skin. Standing up, he dusted off his pants bottoms, then invited the girl to get up, taking one of her baby hands in his. Her strong grip was mildly surprising; he didn't notice how, but as she rose to her feet she broke the bottle against the nearest leg of the swing. Big Chuck expected her to drop it, but she held onto the neck of the bottle, plus the remaining three or four inches of shattered green glass. As he dusted off her behind, whisking away the dead grass with his free hand, Big Chuck suggested, "Why don't we throw that in the Dumpster?"

"Uh-uh, I like blowing on the top." Big Chuck had to laugh. Some of these kids said the damnedest things, not even knowing what it sounded like.

"You like uhm...blowing on it, huh?" he asked as he steered her to the nearby shrubs—after glancing back at the booths, to make sure none of the adults were watching—and she looked up at him, plastic purse in her opposite hand, replying in an oddly-flat voice, "Yeah, blowing is fun," as she followed him into the surrounding dusty green bushes.

Big Chuck thought he'd wear a hole clear through the quarter he was rubbing when she said that. This one might be worth a couple quarters, he thought, keeping that neat row of baby teeth in mind.

* * * * * * *

Amanda had to spit on her tiny hands a few times, the saliva glistening golden-clear in the ever-lowering sunlight, before wiping them off—first on the leaves around her, and then on her underpants—before she closed her bulging purse with a click. As she looped the strap over her wrist, she wished that she'd been able to find a bigger kiddie purse, one with a little more room inside, but the pink vinyl jobbie was the best she could find in the children's section. She would've liked to have used one of her own purses, but they all looked so adult—despite their scaled-down size—that they just wouldn't have been right. Bad enough she'd had to buy herself a damned sun dress, like a six-year-old.

And ankle socks—Amanda's mouth twisted into a bitter *moue*. But Big Chuck had like them, oh yes indeed. Liked the socks and the cotton picot panties enough to show her his first, after she told him she didn't think Funland was all that much fun....

Amanda checked the seams of the pink purse; the lining was all one piece, a molded pouch of paisley-patterned plastic, like a thick sandwich bag molded into the purse, but she couldn't be too careful.

She knew from her observation of the rug rats who frequented this dump of an amusement park that they wouldn't come looking for their over-grown playmate, not while he was "busy"...and once the big kiddies noticed that Mr. Collegiate was missing, she'd be long gone, along with the rest of the carny.

Amanda knew that her suntan would prove just how easy she'd been taking things during her sick leave; hadn't they told her to take it easy, get lots of sun? She'd meet up with one of the advance men tonight, catch a few connecting rides until she was back with the show. First she'd ditch the kiddie clothes and the cheapo plastic handbag—once she put its contents on ice, prior to curing them properly in a salt box.

Behind "Amanda the Amazing" ("Three Feet of Pure Woman!"), Funland was winding down for the afternoon; the golden air rang with childish shouts and the tinny music of the nickel-a-throw rides. The cloying smell of candy and popcorn masked the faint reek of what was stuffed in her purse (she'd actually had to fold it, with a wormy squish that more amused than sickened her) as Amanda casually left the bushes, oblivious to the buzzing drone of the flies already settling on Big Chuck. There were ants, too, but at least they were quiet.

It was only a short walk to the motel room she'd rented; her real clothes were there, some in suitcases, others laid across the bed. Close to the ice bucket she'd asked for that morning, the one waiting to be filled. And then she'd get the ice.

"You don't like Funland very much, do you?" he'd asked, before unzipping, and before she came forward, bottle in hand, points out.

"No, I don't," she said now, softly. She hadn't said anything before, in the bushes. Big Chuck bored her, and she hadn't had much to say to him.

Big Chuck, thinking he was so unique, thinking he was so

special. Big man off campus, with his pocket full of quarters. Quarters. Like it was some big deal. Earn a shiny quarter to spend at good old Funland.

"I could've bought and sold you ten times over, Big Chuck," she whispered to herself, as she crossed an intersection, the slightly warm plastic bag banging against her skin as she walked. "In hundred dollar bills, Big Boy."

Once it was properly cured—a trick she'd learned on the farm, before summer years ago when she'd gone to see a carnival and joined it by nightfall, back when she was a mere teenager—Amanda thought she might hang it above her little bed in the trailer, as a reminder to the apple knockers who lingered to catch her show after the show, a warning not to get too rough. If she felt like it, she might tell them she'd *bitten* it off, and not mention the soda bottle at all. The thought of seeing their shocked, not-wanting-to-believe faces was worth a week spent in a dive like Funland, wasting her vacation doing work, and low-level sideshow stuff at that.

But Amanda was smiling as she opened her motel room door. Mr. Collegiate wasn't lying. Big Chuck *indeed*....

AFTERWORD

This was another one of those story ideas which I had, and then felt compelled to utilize at least twice; the first version I wrote, "At the Playground by..." was part of a cycle of fantasy/ sf stories concerning time travel and famous/infamous people which will appear in a future Borgo Press collection. That story was also published in a very small press zine, much like the one this one appeared in, *Red Eft*. This time around, I decided to go with a straight non-fantasy take on the basic plotline—I like both versions, but this one is a bit more visceral and "grotty."

Amanda here is much more like me as a child; I was a total freak in so many ways—I had (undiagnosed) Asperger's Syndrome, dyslexia (also undiagnosed), and premature puberty (which made me look like an adult when I was nine, so much so that my elementary school demanded to see my birth certificate because they didn't believe how old I really was). I was socially isolated by my family due to their having taken me away from my home state at the age of three in order to get me away from my father—an illegal move, since my mother's sole custody of me had been revoked by a judge, so I was kidnapped before he could claim me—so, in order to make sure I wasn't sent back to Illinois, I wasn't even allowed to know the name of the state where I was born (they called it "back East"). I wasn't allowed to play with anyone outside of school, nor was I ever allowed to even walk outside of our apartment alone, and...on top of all that, I was overweight and ugly, to the point that the other children and even many of my teachers openly ridiculed me in and out of class. I remember one time, in the fifth grade, when we were in the school gym square-dancing, only I was so weird-looking, none of the boys wanted to even touch me when we were doing that hand-off thing during the dance, and the ones who had on long sleeves pulled them over their hands so they wouldn't have to touch me, but the boys with short sleeves began yelling and shouting that they shouldn't have to touch me if the other boys didn't have to—and the teacher, a balding, sourpussed worthless loser of an "educator," chose to do *nothing* to stop what was going on. He just told *me* to keep dancing, and didn't say one freaking *word* to any of those boys to *stop* what they were doing and start behaving. By that time, I was bawling and sobbing, begging this man to please make them stop torturing me, to please, *please* just let me sit this dance out, but the teacher was adamant—I was to just keep on dancing. To this day, I *loathe* dancing. (The same teacher also pulled a reverse of his plan-of-inaction when a girl in my class—after being appointed one of the two captains for the dodge ball teams during another phys ed session—figured out that due to having to select team members second rather than first, that she'd be stuck with me on her team. She began crying and begged the teacher to let me sit on the bench, since she knew that if I was on her team, we'd lose. For once I was all for her suggestion, but he ignored her and I ended up on her team, and we lost.) (At the time, I didn't know it, but girls/women with Asperger's tend to be more clumsy than most people, due to the faulty wiring in the brain.)

I have so many stories about things which were done to me by kids and teachers when I was in elementary school that I could probably write an entire book just listing what happened to me. In short, I was bullied, mercilessly, and it continued all the way through college—once, several classmates of mine cornered me and demanded that I start wearing my hair different ways; they said they couldn't understand how anyone could wear their hair one way day in, day out for months at a time. I mean, this was *college*, and these women had nothing better to occupy their pea brains than to insult me about my hair-do choice. I don't think I had much of anything to do with those women after that—their gall and sheer stupidity was a complete turn-off.

Anyhow...much of the early dialogue in this story was taken almost verbatim from things said to me by fellow students and even teachers when I was in grades one through five; once, a teacher harangued me for not using a popular slang word of the time—she wanted to know why I *didn't* use it! I was so radically different from all my classmates, I might as well have been a circus freak, or an alien dropped down from the sky and plunked in the middle of an elementary school Hades. My mother and grandmother only made matters worse; when I had my first period, a couple of days after turning nine (by which time virtually everything associated with puberty had already happened to me, starting at the age of seven-and-a-half), I was told that I was no longer a child, and that I was an adult, and therefore was *not* to read any "children's books," nor was I to think of myself as a child again. That only further alienated me from my peers; I spent so much time crying and ostracized that I was eventually assigned a social worker by the school system—at which point, when they found out about the social worker, my mother and grandmother put their planned move out of state (the heavy smog in the L.A. area was exacerbating a bad case of bronchitis I'd had since I was seven) into overdrive, and hurried me out of school over a month before the end of the school year. I can't prove it, but I suspect that my mother never gave them an address for sending my school transcripts to Wisconsin, since they never arrived here—I think she was trying to prevent me from being scrutinized and tested periodically (I'd be dragged out of class and subjected to what I later learned were tests for autism; both times I was tested in L.A., apparently the results weren't what they expected—at the time, Asperger's wasn't within the scope of the testing process—but I was told both times that I had "failed the relationship part of the test"), but within a couple of years in Wisconsin, I was once again given the same damn test, and once again told that I had "failed" the relationship part of the test. So much for trying to escape destiny.

I do know that I based what the monstrous Big Chuck tries to do to Amanda on what my grandmother actually did to me; I only wish I could've done to her what Amanda does to Big Chuck...save for the whole "trophy" bit of course.

And yes, I know that most little people don't literally look like children, save for their size, but pituitary dwarfism *does* produce some adults who resemble children—*that's* what I was going for here.

YET ANOTHER POISONED APPLE FOR THE FAIRY PRINCESS

Before Bob had a chance to say word one to me that afternoon, I knew that the Nutcracker Sweet had been holding back on him; I could tell from his eyes-averted, head-hanging shamble into the club locker room, that non-look my way that clearly said *Warning: Man who hasn't had a piece entering the room.*

Wondering, what did you do to her this time to make her clamp those legs together? I decided to let him do all the talking; just nod or grunt or uhm-hum sympathetically, while he opened himself wide and let his guts dangle. I'd discovered long before that afternoon that asking Bob what was wrong would only elicit guarded praise for her from him...as if those double-pierced ears of hers could somehow hear him utter so much as one negative word about her miles away.

It was too bad that those bitch-keen ears of hers couldn't pick up the jokes the rest of the guys at the club made about Bob *because* of her; the jokes about Bob, the Ball-less Wonder, or Bob, the amazing Pussy-Man—had to grow his own so he'd get some once in a while—but even if she could've heard them, I doubt that they would've affected her. Not after all the times she'd called him "*stupid*" in front of the entire tennis club during the annual charity matches, or the times she'd told all the other wives how inept and boring his lovemaking was...when and if she decided to allow him into her bedroom. Even though Jeanette made a pretense of speaking oh so softly, her brittle little-girl voice tinkling like wind chimes, that tiny voice had a way of carrying across the courts.

Beside me, Bob tossed his racket and balls into the open locker before him, the metal interior rattled dully, making a sound not unlike two cats trying to hump each other in a Dumpster, just before he slammed the door shut. I calmly began stripping off my whites, concentrating on the knots in my laces while he took off each article of clothing he wore with the sort of seething deliberation that is somehow more furious than flinging away one's shirt, shorts, and socks in open anger. And he folded each piece of clothing the way men who have to do their own laundry do it, before stacking it in a neat, corners-aligned pyramid on the bench before him.

"I have Bob trained," I'd heard Jeanette say on more than one occasion. "I made sure of that after I married him. Just like the other one...he did everything for himself."

Jeanette's first husband sure did do everything for himself—including that final blow job on the business end of his .38. And he was considerate enough to do *that* out in the woods, where he wouldn't mess up her spotless floors or pristine wallpapered walls.

Bob was putting his jockstrap (likewise neatly folded in a tiny soft square) on the very top of his cloth pyramid, a white pinnacle of sweaty elastic, as he finally said, "Y'know, I used to think she was nothing but a witch...but I finally have it figured out."

I grunted sympathetically while scooping up my towel and soap-on-a-rope (rounded globe of tit-shaped pinkish soap, a playful gift from my own girlfriend), before padding off for the showers. No need to ask Bob to follow me, within seconds I could hear the slap-slap of his bare feet smacking against the tile floor. His wife sure did have him trained.

He and I were alone in the locker room/showers. I don't think he would've felt able to speak so freely if the others had been there. I wasn't even sure why he'd picked me to unload on those other times; maybe it was because I was a newcomer to the club and hadn't screwed his wife during those frenzied days between the death of Chump Number One (funny, she'd never mentioned his name—I doubted that even Bob knew it...unless the poor schmuck's folks *did* christen him The Other One) and Chump Number Two. Oh, I'd heard about Jeanette's kiss-by-suck-by-fuck climb up the rungs of the membership ladder; whenever Bob couldn't come to the club, the tiled shower walls rang with the stories of her suction-cup blow-jobs and her vise-like pussy, not to mention the intricate things she could do with her tongue. But her prowess between the sheets (or on the car seat, or under the stars) was her undoing; sure, taking a *piece* of something that all but sucks you dry once in a while is okay, but a steady diet of it would leave a man hollow in a month.

Or worse than hollow. Like The Other One with his permanent skylight on the top of his bloodied head.

All the members of the tennis club—be they single, married, or anything in between—had had her; every man knew the taste of her juices, the smell of her, too, but no matter how perfect her icy-blond hair was, or how carefully she applied those graduated shades of makeup to her otherwise slightly puffy and colorless face (Terry Collier once took a shower with her after an extended session and claimed that she was "almost faceless... just eyes, a lump of nose and a suction hose below that"), eventually the guy would realize that no matter what she looked like, or what she fucked like, he'd have to actually try to live with the prospect which sent the majority of the club members running once they'd satisfied their urges.

Until Bob came along. Nobody knew if it was because he'd been the next best thing to a virgin before meeting her, or if he'd had one of Those mothers who'd given him a taste of the whip across his psyche from boyhood on...but whatever the reason, she hooked him. *Then* she trained him.

Positioning myself under the shower head, I waited until I saw Bob hovering just at the outer reaches of my peripheral vision before turning on the water. As the fine sprinkling of warm water cascaded down my chest, across my belly and block and tackle, Bob's voice started in again, the words barely audible over the splatter of the shower spray hitting my body and the tile floor below.

"It isn't just that witches are supposed to be as ugly as they are powerful...although you wouldn't believe what she looks like without the makeup. 'Course when I was a kid, that's all you ever heard—that witches were so full of power, the power to make people do whatever they want them to do. Witches had command over *themselves*...to fool people, and lure them into doing things. The stories never said anything about their sex lives y'know, as if women that ugly weren't supposed to want any...maybe it was their not ever getting any that made them vulnerable to the fairy princesses. Now *they're* the ones with the real power—"

Caressing my globe of nipple-tipped soap with one wet hand, I worked up a lather while nodding empathetically, all the while fighting the building urge to start caressing myself with my other hand. It wasn't a big deal with the other guys around, but it wasn't the thing to do in front of a guy who was only turning the "cold" knob in front of him and letting the stream of water hit him in his already-drooping organ.

"—how else could they survive all the things the witches did to 'em, unless they had the power? Fairy princesses could consume poison apples like they were only covered with candy. Oh, sure, they'd play at being overcome, for sympathy...only way to lure in the suckers who'd rescue them—"

Smearing frothy lather across my upper body, I grunted in reply while Bob just stood there, wet dick limp, balls retracting like kicked puppies curling themselves into defensive lumps of quivering fear, and continued to speak to the walls which had echoed with recitations of his own "fairy princess's" exploits.

"She claimed that she couldn't find anyone who really loved her. Her first...one didn't. That's why he did what he did. Because he didn't love her. Why he didn't just leave her she never explained...only now she doesn't *need* to.

"I think she did to him what she's doing to me...and after something like *that*, leaving must've seemed impossible. Leaving means needing to explain, needing to answer questions...'How could you give up a body like hers?' 'The way she flirts, she must want it twenty hours at a pop—couldn't keep up, could you?' 'She wear you out, buddy-boy?' Because they all can see what she is, they've all flirted with her...and maybe more. Not that any of 'em will come out and say it, but...I can read their eyes.

"But they don't know...not at all. Sure, she has the legs, and what's between 'em—*if* it suits her. If not...."

Hanging the now-glistening orb of pink soap on the "hot" knob before me, I worked the lather over the rest of my body but did manage to look over at Bob and give him a knowing wink—Sure, pal, every girl pulls the locked-legs bit.

Something in my glance must have connected, for Bob grew slightly agitated, his voice climbing a notch in volume, as he shook his head in protest. "No, no, not just refusing me...it's—it's much more than that. I mean, if she doesn't want me to get some, I *can't*...you can't get what isn't there at all. All I have to do is say something she doesn't like or fail to do something she asked me to, and"—here he sucked in his lips until his mouth was merely an indented line hovering on the horizontal under his nose—"*nothing*. Gone...no way to get your fingers or tongue or anything in...not when there's no hole to stick 'em *in*to."

My eyes must've registered my disbelief, for at that point Bob shut off his own water, and as he stood there dripping and shivering slightly, he continued, "I'm not kidding...she can pull everything *in*, lips, hair, the works. It's more than muscle control...no sexercise book for women can teach her *that*. Maybe it's instinctive—maybe it's something she learned on her own. One minute you're curling her hair around your finger, brushing against her wet lips...and the next, it's like...nothing. Just rubbing a patch of flat flesh on her belly. And the worst part is, how she smiles when she's doing it, just that little tug at the corners of her mouth while her eyes just stare into you.

"Course, it's not something you can ask a marriage counselor or sex therapist about. Because she'd never admit it...and who wants to look like a nut? And I've looked in the medical books... no woman has that many muscles there, to be able to do *that*.

"But a fairy princess...now *she'd* be able to do that. *Would* do that. How else could a fairy princess stay alive when someone's trying to poison her? All she'd have to do is close up something inside, and keep the poison away from her insides. If she can do it down there, she can do it anyplace on her body."

As Bob blathered on, his words trickling like drops of water until the individual droplets formed a small yet mighty flood, I remembered what some of the guys had had to say about his "fairy princess":

"I'd of sworn she was going to slurp out every drop from both balls, she was sucking on me like my dong was a straw and my whole body was the cup holding the milkshake—"

"Remember those woven thingies you'd stick your fingers in, and then the more you'd pull to get free, the faster you'd be stuck? Well, stick hair on one end, and you've got her."

"She was *all* mouth, like she'd suck your lungs out if you let 'er—"

But that's just shower-room talk, I assured myself. And Bob's so starved for a little pussy he's starting to think there isn't any to be had...if he lets himself think about what he's missing, he'll really go nuts. If the food isn't there, you won't be hungry.

"—after the first few times, when I managed to reach over and turn the lights on before she completely pulled herself in, just so I could *see* it happening, I decided that she couldn't do it everywhere at once, so I'd reposition myself, dangle the bait over her other lips...but all she had to do was say very softly, 'No, I don't *think* so,' in that tiny voice of hers, and I'd start to get just as small as her voice down there. Couldn't even prime the pump with my hands afterward. Like...just her voice had been enough to keep me from firming up."

I'd heard that "tiny voice" many a time, her *matte* finish

lipsticked lips barely moving as that terse voice nonetheless blasted the air, sending shattering waves of sound rippling outward:

"Bob, you're so *stupid*—"

"The man can't do anything right—"

"The only way to live with a man is to keep him on his own side of the bed as much as possible—"

And that's just supreme-bitch talk, I thought; thousands of other women say the same things, while their men grovel and scrape and put up with it in the hopes of being rewarded with a blow job and a little action afterwards...isn't it?

"—'course, what she can do to herself, and to my body, that's temporary, but what happened to my stuff, now that, *that's* another story altogether," Bob was saying, and at that point, as the soap foam dried with small popping and snapping sounds on my damp body, I reached over and shut off my own mix of hot and cold water. With the sound of the rushing water gone, Bob's words echoed sharply on the steamy white tiles:

"She uses her voice...only, when she's really angry, it doesn't stay tiny or soft. Y'know how a dental drill seems to get louder and louder as it comes closer to your mouth, until the sound is *everything*? Just that persistent *drone*? She's something like that...only more. I can tell when it'll happen now—her voice goes all sharp and flat at once, and she says my name like it's so much longer than it is: 'Baaahh—ob' before she really gets going.

"Once, we were in the car, I was driving, only she didn't like the way I was driving; she always says I drive too slow, 'pokey,' as she puts it, and she goes 'Baaahh—ob, put your *foot* on the pedal, don't play footsies with it, *stomp* it,' only she was speaking too high to get the pedal itself...but when my fingers started to sink into the steering wheel, I knew I'd better get the car moving. It took weeks for the plastic to go back to normal....I stayed away from the club for all that time, because I was afraid someone might see what happened to the wheel and ask what happened.

"Maybe it's their voices...maybe fairy princesses can shatter anything that might hurt them, neutralize the poisons in the apple, y'know? Those tight little voices, aimed right at a man... or anything he cares about. Tiny, brittle voices, like glass knives or crystal daggers...hard, tight voices with no softness in them. Like when she pulls herself *in*, and doesn't leave a bit of softness or moisture...and she doesn't even have to close herself up to stop me; I can actually be in her, working up a steady rhythm, then it sort of skids to a stop, no lubrication, you see... dry and rigid and unmoving, like trying to hump the hole in a bowling ball, only it's *not* something funny"—he'd noticed the slight smirk on my lips—"not at all...and she can make her mouth go dry, too, as if she'd never been able to so much as spit in her entire life. Can you imagine sticking your tongue into a parchment envelope? It doesn't even *taste* like anything. Same goes for the other set of lips. One second, she's a mass of petals and honey, the next—like I'm licking envelope flaps without the glue on them. Worse than nothing. Not even an unpleasant taste in my mouth to complain about afterwards."

I dipped my head to one side, frowning slightly in agreement. Even a slightly salty clam has its appeal, even if that appeal is in the complaining about it afterwards. But to experience... nothing? Not even the smell—

As if sensing my flow of thought, Bob leaned forward and went on. "And she won't even allow herself to give off so much as the odor of sweat if she feels I don't deserve to smell her. I suspect it's because that's something about her that I could appreciate without her actually offering it to me, or dangling it like a prize—the brass ring she can keep holding just out of reach. Now it's like...I'm not worth teasing...."

Momentarily thankful that Bob had stopped speaking, I quickly turned on the "hot" knob and allowed the water to pummel my skin, rinsing away the drying soap film and Bob's strange words, which seemed almost to cling to my body like a coating of scum.

But my sense of release was short-lived; Bob simultaneously

grabbed his bar of deodorant soap and raised his voice while resuming his low-key rant as he lathered his body with sharp, jerking motions of his soap-clutching hand.

"I guess this fairy princess has had her lifetime fill of sympathy, or whatever it is she needs....I'm not even allowed to enter her bedroom anymore. Not that she doesn't need stimulation anymore—I can hear that vibrator of hers buzzing through the bedroom wall.... Apparently, she likes something she can manipulate at will. I've seen that thing, when she's out of the house and doesn't know I'm in her bedroom. She's...melted it, compressed it in spots, to conform to her own cunt.... From the little I can remember of it now, I'd say she's turned that trusty vibrator into an exact match to her hole, bump by bump, all the way to the hilt. Like fucking herself *with* herself.... I wonder, sometimes, if she'd have done that to me by now, if I'd pleased her enough for her to allow me to continue bedding down with her. Reshaped me to suit her needs, like a flesh-and-blood French tickler. No, not a good idea," he said, almost to himself. "She'd be leaving herself open to too much scrutiny. If it's one thing that fairy princesses must do, it's protect their powers, not let people really know what they're capable of...not unless the person witnessing them is so beneath contempt that *no* one would believe them.

No matter how bizarre his excuse for not getting laid was, that part of Bob's story rang true. The Amazing Pussy-Man was the ultimate joke at the tennis club; by that time, all someone had to do was mention his name, and that utterance would be greeted with snorts of derision and hoots of laughter. Bob had become the prince to his wife's Nutcracker; all she had to do was move those hinged, clicking jaws, and presto—instant eunuch. I glanced over and down; sure enough, his nuts were trying to re-enter the shell of his body, while his dick dangled like a defeated worm. I was almost tempted to take a second look, but didn't want Bob thinking I was going strange on him... but didn't it used to be a bit *longer* when flaccid?

Once Bob finished soaping himself, and his skin was covered

with a mucus-like filmy coating of tiny-bubbled soap, he looked me in the eye and said, "I'm not just blowing steam.....Jeanette *is* a fairy princess. If she was a witch, like so many women are, I would leave her in a minute. Let her have everything, pay her off for life. But doing that would just free her up, let her start searching and hunting again. Like what happened after the other one...y'know. At least he was able to taste something in his mouth before he did it.

"Taste or not, though. I don't want to do that—"

Beside him, I nodded vigorously and gave a snort of affirmation, sort like the "good boy" noise you'd make when dealing with an obedient dog.

"—but leaving a fairy princess like her isn't easy no matter which way you go about it. Stay with her, and you might as well be alone. Leave her, and you wonder who she'll be trapping next. It's not ethical, y'know, knowingly doing that to another man."

"Uh-uh," I answered, thinking of all the would-be prey that had escaped her clawed clutches before Bob came along.

"Especially after what she did to me yesterday. I was about to pleasure myself in my bedroom, but when I reached over for the bottle of lotion I keep in my headboard bookcase, I knocked over the open bottle, and it was all curdled, like it'd spoiled or gone rotten, which was nuts, because all it *is* is a bunch of oils— safflower, soy, palm, stuff like that, with some vitamin E mixed in. So there I was, looking at the cheesy clumps of the stuff spilled all over my pillow, when *she* walks past my bedroom door and says through it, 'What do you want to use *that* for?' Just like that. Like either she'd been nosing around in my room, or she'd seen me through the wall and the door.

"Her grubbing through my stuff I could take—I do it to her, after all—but for her to go...changing everything of mine, especially when she dries *herself* up in the first place"—here Bob slathered the soap around his already withered organ with a vigor born not of self-love, but of self-loathing—"and then won't let *me* have any lubrication for myself!"

I clucked my tongue in condolence as I hurried up and toweled myself off, hoping I could get dry fast enough to get back into my own street clothes, and then out of there before Bob finished his own shower. Yet, even though his words were growing stranger, something in his voice compelled me to stay. I don't know if it was the raw pain, or the first glimmers of regained self-respect in his words, but instead of hurrying out of there, I found myself lingering. And seeing that his audience wasn't about to leave, Bob placed his soap on the small shelf before him and stood under the pulsing stream of water, poking his head under the spray until his dark hair covered his skull in a flat, shiny layer, conforming to the rounded contours of his head like the shiny skin on an apple, as he concluded softly:

"While I was looking at that spilled mess on my pillow, I got to thinking. If she can do something like this to a fluid, what might she do to the fluids inside of *me*? Did she turn the other one's blood to something that poisoned him, *made* him do what he did out there in the woods? Because if she *can* do that, just like she can melt things or suck them in, there's not escaping her—even for a guy like *you*, someone who's been *warned*, once she gets it into her mind to actually *go* for someone—at least not while she's up and moving. But what to do with a fairy princess like her? Give her yet another poisoned apple? She'd just eat it to the core and go looking for more. By the way, have I ever told you that she finds you quite attractive? Claims she like the 'quiet type.' So...I got to thinking, maybe poisoned apples, things like that, aren't the answers...not unless you add a little more poison to the apple, whatever. Maybe...someone—or a couple of somebody's—might have to do *something* else to her, even be a little less insidious, a little less subtle. Y'know what I mean. Only question is, would you be willing to be the one to help me add a little more poison to the apple—or what*ever*?"

I hugged my towel against my body, unable to answer him, even though I'd understood the question perfectly. And, as if realizing that despite the fact that the question was received, it couldn't *yet* be acknowledged. Bob added, his eyes (for once) level with my own, "I'm not just asking you because you haven't fucked her yet...it's because she *has* noticed you already, and, well, being married to The Other One didn't stop her from roaming and looking and *tainting* other men. Given her interest in you, it would be so simple to just let her *go* for you—and no matter what you might think you could do, I doubt you'd have much more luck resisting her than I did. But then again, The Other One never tried to stop her, or even so much as warn the others...like I'm warning *you.* Not that I could stop her if she does decide to try for you...but a warning is a warning. And maybe the two of us could turn a warning into an end to a need for all future warning about her. I'm only doing this for *your* sake. Won't you do something for yourself, while you still can? Or, if not for yourself, then for the next chump she'll adhere to after *you*?"

That speech called for more than a grunt or a nod or an "uh-huh" or "uh-uh." With a few sentences, a scattering of casually uttered syllables, Bob had crossed over from speculation to supposition to surety. But warning to me or not, I didn't think I was ready to follow him *that* far into his personal plan for combined revenge and prevention—so I began to slowly shake my head no (after all, I could always find another tennis club, in another town) when the moist echoing stillness of the shower room was shattered by the shrill jangle of the phone in the locker room a few feet away. Since I was basically dried off, I wrapped my towel around my waist and padded, my soles smacking against the damp tiles like dozens of loud kisses, over to the ringing phone.

I heard Jeanette's voice the second I lifted the receiver, even before I'd had a chance to place it against my ear and mouth:

"Baaahh-ob? Is Bob there? I have to speak with him. Baaah—"

Her voice was almost loud enough for him to hear without coming any closer to the phone, but he did so anyway, walking head down and privates bobbing in time with his slow, defeated steps forward. But just as I was about to hand the receiver to him, I happened to glance at the earpiece, in time to see the formerly tiny holes dilate, then close with infinitesimal slowness after her voice had blasted through the tortured, malleable plastic—and before I gave him the still-contracting receiver, I realized that a fairy princess *that* powerful, that...*omnipotent*... might very well find a way to do anything to me, to *any* of the men at the tennis club (or *beyond* the confines of this club), *especially* when she found herself free of Bob. And Bob was so close to unleashing her, either intentionally or by accident (yet he did say *she* found *me* appealing...*me*, she'd specifically singled *me* out), and if he was subjected to even one more indignity—so, as I handed the receiver to him, I managed to catch his eye before I reluctantly nodded yes to his question about me helping to add more poison—or something less subtle but more foolproof under out combined effort—to that apple.

AFTERWORD

This really isn't my favorite story out of all the stories I've written. Aside from the fact that it originally appeared in an anthology whose editors treated me like a fifth-rate hack whose input they sought only because someone had suggested to them that they include more female writers in their latest anthology (and who were so unimpressed when the story was chosen for *The Year's Best Fantasy and Horror* that they never even mentioned the honor to me, or saw fit to congratulate me), I'm personally not very big on fairy tales myself. I wasn't encouraged to read them when I was young, and until I discovered the unaltered, darker original versions of the Grimm Brothers' tales when I was an adult, the obligatory happy endings didn't cut it for me. I knew how hideous and pointless life could be from an early age, so the concept of happily-ever-after was nothing but a sham for me.

But, to get to the genesis of this particular story, it's based on several women I've known, all of whom were ball-busters, nutcrackers, you name it: They loved to emotionally castrate men. And denying sexual favors was a common ploy among them, which I took to the next (and possibly ultimate) level here. While I'm extremely aware of how rotten some men can be to women, I also know just how hideously vicious women can be to men—and how they can get away with a heck of a lot by virtue of being female. (Or, as Robert Heinlein once said, "Don't let them give you to the women"....) And extremely good-looking women seem most able to dish out the worst to men, since they can get away with it, again by virtue of their looks. (I've never had that "problem" myself—I was always considered to be the ugliest girl in my particular class, all the way through college. So there wasn't much of anything I was able to gain by virtue of my looks, such as they weren't.)

Although the character of Bob is certainly a door-mat, I do feel rather sorry for him. And I hope that he and the narrator would be able to get away with killing this particular Fairy Princess. Geeze, she's asking for it....

...AND DO IT AGAIN

(Dedicated to Dave Foley)

"What serial killers do is they try to get it right. You
go back to where it hurts; you do it over and over."
—Joseph Stefano, screenwriter, *Psycho*
(in *Premiere*, October 1993)

My next maybe-she-would-be, maybe-she-wouldn't victim
paused for a second to adjust her sunglasses before walking
around the back of my car to the passenger-side door, just long
enough for her to take in the customization on my license plate.
Not that it mattered about her *seeing* it, for all I cared, she could
whip out her Yuppie-essential Powerbook from her genuine
calfskin purse (you can always tell real leather handbags by
their smell), and file away my license-plate number...after all,
depending on how things went, within an hour or so she'd be
yet another lifeless hunk of flesh and seeping blood bundled
up in the thick motel-issue shower curtains (they hose off in
seconds once I get tired of carting my last victim around) in the
trunk of said car, her head resting mere inches from my just-
slightly-altered license plate, but all she *did* do was execute a
half-turn on her matching calf-skin-covered sling-back pumps,
and then bend down closer to the back fender, to take a confirm-
ing look at the plate.

Considering the cut of her clothes, and the exquisite sense
of taste she displayed in her choice of accessories (RayBans®,

Hermes scarf, golden double-drop-off earrings), it rather did surprise me that she was one of those people who mouth words as they read them.

The majority of my victims aren't as *gauche*....

Rising to her feet in a swirling ripple of wool challis "carwash" double-paneled, multi-layered skirt, gently-shifting draped scarf and perfectly-coifed, wavy caramel-colored hair (the sound of her skirt alone, the fabric rubbing against itself, almost made my knees buckle with anticipation), she asked, "Why in the world would Wisconsin put 'America's *Dahmer*land' at the bottom of their plates? It seems to me they'd rather forget *that*...episode."

Before she noticed "America's Dahmerland" had been painstakingly painted *over* the regulation logo "America's Dairyland" along the bottom of my standard-issue deep-red-over-white plates, I quickly walked around the front of my car, and opened the passenger-side door for her.

"Oh, it's simply an effort to appreciate their cannibals...no doubt the legislators noticed how much the citizens of Colorado seem to enjoy the legacy of Alfred Packer—those tee shirts and film festivals and all—and decided to finally cash in on a recent state serial killer. After all, Ed Gein was long dead by then," I replied with cheerful aplomb, as she gracefully eased herself into the car, and tucked her silk-hosed legs in with that effortless, intrinsically feminine swing up-and-over that invariably sets my killing hand to aching, with that anticipatory longing— as if it were already gripping the handle of my ax, just prior to the first over-and-down arc of the blade, followed by that initial lubricating splash of blood to warm and smooth out the slightly-raised grain of the wood—

But that was a pleasure which would simply have to wait— if it was even going to happen at all this time—at least until I managed to get the car started, and drive out of the restaurant parking lot. I've found—sometimes to my chagrin—that the other patrons don't appreciate dripping smears of blood on their windshields...at least not the type of people who habitually frequent four-star restaurants....

Once I'd hurried back around to the driver's-side door, and let myself into the car, she half-turned her head my way (keeping one shaded eye on the reflection of herself in the mirror mounted outside the passenger-side door), and replied, "I suppose it's better than putting that ubiquitous *cow* of theirs on the plates, the way they do on the lottery scratch-off tickets. Imagine, a cow wearing *sun*glasses...."

"Uh-hum," I muttered, still keeping my voice cheerfully noncommittal as I reached over and turned on the in-dash CD player (I'd recently had to upgrade my system; some of my victims found my old cassette player too *passé* for their rarefied tastes...although I'd yet to need to upgrade my choice of weapon). My favorite album from my high-school days was already loaded in the system: *Countdown to Ecstasy*, by Steely Dan, and naturally I had my signature song keyed up and ready to start the second I hit the button—that ode to every psycho-sexual killer alive, "Razor Boy."

(Oh, not that I'd ever stoop to using a razor on one of my victims. Too much chance of coming into pre-kill contact with warm, resisting flesh. And certainly too much of a chance of them getting close enough to grab *me* by the wrist or sleeve....)

Beside me, she shifted around in her seat, trying to pull the seat-belt-shoulder-harness over her torso, but no matter how hard she pulled it wouldn't reach down far enough (certainly not after I'd customized the straps, making sure they *wouldn't* stretch far enough...it's bad enough wiping bloodstains off a leather-covered car seat; trying to clean those straps *is* murder), so after a few more seconds of struggling, the rasping, almost frantic susurration of fine fabrics rubbing and scarping against each other boring right into my psyche, despite the six-speakers-amplified song filling the car, she ultimately turned to me with an apologetic half-smile on her impeccably-painted lips, and said, "Do you mind if I ride *sans* a seatbelt? If it bothers you, I could cab home—"

Even if I said I did mind if she went without a seatbelt, I knew she wouldn't bother hiring a cab. I knew her type; spend

spend spend her money for nonsensical baubles, for disgustingly expensive meals, but balk at giving a grubby cabby so much as a dime tip. So much better to hitch a ride home with a like-dressed member of their own sub-species (*homo affluentus*, perhaps?), preferably a suitably innocuous-looking male dining on his lonesome at a table for two...the kind of harmless-seeming, albeit lonely-looking lawyer-doctor-CEO type I happen to be. So much better to be seen with the likes of me than to sit in displaced misery in the back of some cigarette-stale taxi cab.

Although I do wonder—how do these lost luxuriant souls get *to* the restaurants without their car? Not that I stick around to find out any answers....

"Doesn't matter to me...personally, I find it difficult to back out of a driveway wearing one myself. Tends to play hell with my suit jackets." Next to me, she let out a small cultured sigh of relief, as she let go of the offending shoulder harness (it retracted with a *zuuup* of harsh-sounding webbing that set my teeth on edge—*not* a sensual sound at all) before patting the outer, hanging panels of her camel-colored shirt into place over her decorously crossed-at-the-calves knees. Unobtrusively, I turned down the volume of the stereo (the song was almost over anyhow) so I wouldn't miss the faint rustle of the layers of fine fabric shifting over each other, and the silken hose beneath....

"I couldn't agree with you more...I could almost spit when I see those dry-cleaning bills. It's almost enough to make me invest in a bottle of Woolite...."

Almost, but not quite, eh? I told myself, as I shifted the car into second gear and quitted the parking lot; as much as I loathe her kind, they do give me a certain pleasure—aside from hacking them apart, that is—I suppose you could say it's the inherent dichotomy...exquisite exteriors vs. petty, self-righteous interiors. Cuts down on *my* feelings of albeit minimal guilt later on...although any guilt I *do* feel is entirely due to needing to wreck their clothing while killing them. Especially after I gain so much pre-kill pleasure from listening to the twills, gabardines and pure silk chiffons sing to me, whisper such indecent secrets with each movement of the wearer; barely-voiced tales of longing and wanting and promised fulfillment which completely contradict the empty words spoken by the wearer. And, conveniently for me, the susurration is unisexual; crossed trouser legs and silk neckties sliding across lightly starched cotton shirt-fronts sing equally enticing songs to me...especially if I listen selectively, and tune out their idle prattle.

"—to that album all the time when I was in school, too," the woman was saying, her natural voice barely audible over the rising song of her shifting paneled skirt, and her whispering draped scarf.

I do hate it when this happens. Bad enough that they bore me with tales of their meaningless, extremely well-paid jobs in the restaurants and high-class bars; for the record, I've killed lawyers, doctors (specialists, mostly), several rising executive types, and even a couple of CEO's—one of them a woman—but it's far more difficult for me to match a life-story with a body than to remember specific articles of clothing they'd worn. A supple William Morris tie, half-hidden behind a single-breasted Italian-silk suit-coat, or the subtle play of light over the ever-moving surface of a velvet blazer with glinting, reflective satin lapels...now *those* are silent stories worth remembering. Bad enough that I have to look my soon-to-be-victim (or victims— I've taken many a couple for that last, elegant ride home) in the eye, while nodding politely as they pontificate over their pork chops in aspic or whatever Yuppie edible is currently "In," and interjecting whatever appropriate monosyllables are necessary to keep them from losing interest in me and toddling home without me.

"Did anyone in your crowd get in trouble for playing that killer song?" I definitely hate it when the victims start *asking* me things; aside from the obligatory "Are you dining alone? Would you mind some company?" I mentally recoil from questions... after all, it's enough of a momentary betrayal when one seemingly of your kind pulls out his trusty ax and begins swiping away at you, without adding the indignity of that person you *know something about*, and vice-versa, killing you.

"Uh-uh." I hoped that would pacify her; keeping one eye on the passing street signs, I felt along the dashboard until I found the heater knob, and switched it on. Initially, the warm air filling the passenger compartment does the most wonderful things to quiescent fabric; skirts rustle, ties flutter, and always there's the added movement as arms reach down or across to smooth down the disturbed garments. But this one wasn't going to take "Uh-uh" for an answer....

"Oh? You must've gone to a rather liberal school...at *my* high school, anyone caught with a copy of that album was sent home immediately. It was worse when that third Led Zeppelin album came out, remember the one with the movable disk under the cover, the one you could spin around to form a new picture under those cut-out circles on the top of the cover? Anyone caught playing with *that* during study hall was marched down to the vice-principal's office *pronto*. Of course, we students managed to get even...during lunch time we could bring our own records and singles to play in the cafeteria, and once we played Nazareth's "Love Hurts" over and *over* for an hour-and-a-half—"

I wished she'd stop, just as I wished I could simply stop listening to her words, her petty little memories...not merely because they *were* so trivial, so juvenile, but because they *were* so real.

No, I would've told her, if I wasn't so intent on trying to lose myself in the fiber-and-movement-and-understated-elegance song of her garments, *No, I didn't come from a liberal school at all. I came from a place where other kids like you wouldn't have even waster your precious, self-absorbed time bothering me or noticing that I was alive. I could've slit your throat from ear-to-ear in front of all of them without so much as eliciting a response. Not as long as I was considered to be a nothing, a nobody who couldn't afford to dress like all the other kids, a nonentity who wasn't worth the energy to hate, let alone acknowledge as a fellow human being.*

Glancing down at my own suit, my own tie (well, *now* my own; the Yuppie lawyer—or was he an accountant?—I'd killed a few days ago certainly wasn't going to miss the clothes I grabbed from his overstocked closet), noting with painful satisfaction that they were easily as elegant as those articles of clothing *she* wore, I wondered if she'd be sitting here, "*sans*" seatbelt and shoulder harness, in my car, allowing me to chauffeur her to her in-all-probability $500-a-month apartment, if I wasn't superficially just like *her*; tailored, natural-fabrics-only clothes, perfectly groomed hair, animal-rights-activists-be-damned leather shoes, and a subtle miasma of beyond-expensive aftershave (likewise filched from the marble-countered two-sink bathroom of my latest victim—can't recall the name, but the bottle is huge, faceted and ostentatious to the *max*). Oh, of course it helps that I have hair that isn't quite blonde or brown, but that certain "medium" shade that every other Caucasian person walking down the street in any town or city seems to have, and that my eyes are just blue—not Paul Newman bright—just smokily grayish-blue enough to be unremarkable, or that my features are even and unobtrusive enough not to attract over-attention...or *pique* the memories of any potential witnesses in the restaurants, cocktail lounges or parking lots.

Give me the right camouflage, and I'm irresistible. I never have to seek out my victims; not a one. As long as I act the perfect vacuum, a well-dressed, perfectly-groomed void waiting for some unsuspecting victim to temporarily fill me up.... And fill me up they do, from the moment they begin to move my way, making fine fabric rub against itself with their passage, a small, intense sound audible over the noisiest of dining or drinking places; I feel myself growing full from that first moment of contact, until the last moment when their blood trickles over their bodies and their clothing, and I hear that last liquid note of satisfied longing.... Once that happens, I'm quite full...even as the emptying process begins anew. (Oh, for a song of silk and velvet and gabardine that merely stays a solo, uninterrupted by those discordant, empty descants of questions and idle prattle....).

But there almost always comes a point where the would-be victim becomes the certain-to-be victim; the questions, the joking asides, the intimate *details*, manage to drown out the sensual silken sounds, until all I'm left with is an irritation to my sight and hearing, something I need to switch off, like a radio....

Even if the act of switching them off becomes a pleasure in itself. There's always that longing for that uninterrupted melody; the prospect of just sitting by that person's silent side, listening to the way each inhalation and exhalation sets up infinitesimal ripples and sighs of fabric rubbing fabric, just seems to somehow elude me, though.

"—at your school?" Damn; I hadn't heard the question, and I wasn't close enough to her apartment house to let the query go unanswered, or—worse yet—answered incorrectly. Instinctively pressing buttons on my CD player, until I'd re-keyed "Razor Boy," I casually asked, "Pardon? I was so busy looking at street signs, I missed the question—"

"I *said*, were you the only Steely Dan fan at your school? Or were there other potential subversives lurking in those hallowed halls?" Great. Now I had to answer *two* questions...and given her instructions as to where her apartment building was located, I'd have another ten minutes to fill up with minimal conversation. I glanced over at her; from the bemused expression on her face, I surmised that she meant the second question as a joke. No need to take her—or the question—seriously.

(Getting this small-talk thing right is even more difficult than knowing just how to accessorize an Italian silk suit without looking like a pimp, or knowing when to stop splashing on some dead accountant/lawyer's purloined aftershave. No matter how inane *their* words were, my potential victims are quite sensitive when it comes to picking up *my* verbal *faux pas*....)

"I seem to remember that there were only five or six of us...the janitor's room where we held our meetings was always dark." There. Both questions killed with one sentence. Her unaffected laughter in reply indicated that my response was satisfactory. But then she had to go and *do* it again—

"I was the only one who was *really* into them, aside from the shock value and all...it was like, what they'd written was for me, like it spoke to me alone. Which is silly...but ever since I first heard 'Do It Again,'" I felt like someone was singing something *I* could...*cherish*, y'know, like a friend who knew me and still didn't care about my peculiarities or whatnot. Like they understood that life wasn't all drippy ballads like 'Love Hurts,' songs that *pretended* to know what alienation and *angst* were about, but boiled down to the same old clap-trap. When Fagen hurt, *I* hurt, too, and...this may sound funny, but it was *good* to hurt like that—"

No, no, no, I countered mentally, as my hands gripped the steering wheel so hard I could hear the slippery *scrish* of moist flesh meeting unyielding leather, *it's* never *good to hurt like that. Sure, it's comforting to know that someone empathizes with your pain, but that'll never take it away.* That's *the beauty of the music...that those hurtful things* are, *and need not be justified. You want music that* really *soothes you, you go make it happen...or get in tune with the subtle music happening all around you. Savor the irony that the ones you detest the most make the sweetest music of all, the most* sensual, *subtle private music. And revel in the added irony that what sets them apart from what you* really *are provides that thrill you can't buy—*

What was quite revealing about her little speech was the way remembering her past made her a part of it; the high-school-girl "y'knows" and the meandering syntax...with a softly-voiced sigh, I told myself this wouldn't be one of those complete, fulfilling kills, when I got all the way into her apartment, maybe listened to some more idle, albeit polished, chatter over tiny sparkling glasses of liquors poured from faceted, stoppered, for-show bottles, before making some plausible excuse to go out to my car and retrieve whatever thing in there I'd conned the victim into wanting to see, then savoring that swift "oh!" of stunned disbelief when the victim and/or *victims* saw the darkly blood-daubed ax in my neatly-manicured hands. I knew that if I continued this ride with *this* one, and even half-listened to what she was saying, as she verbally regressed to a point *I* never wanted to be reminded of again, *ever*, I'd lose all feelings of anticipation, or purely, sexlessly-sartorial desire...and I'd end up letting her live.

Which was not a good idea; she'd seen *and* commented on my self-executed vanity license plate, and might remember other things about me, things which might just filter back into her oddly-adolescent mind should news of one of my later kills reach her mouth-the-words attention. Too bad, really, that she wasn't one of those ultimately-discarded-while-alive victims whose clothes turned out to be albeit convincing-looking/sounding synthetics (in the closer quarter of my car, I can always tell the subtle aural difference); I could actually work up some measure of pity for the trying-to-maintain-the-image ones too busy to keep up the *façade* to notice my designer plates, or cheerfully ghoulish small-talk, so they seldom posed a problem. Kindred souls, I suppose....

Noticing that I was driving through a particularly ill-lit section of her neighborhood (few streetlights shining through the green-turning-to-gold/orange/red leaves on the surrounding trees), I fast-forwarded my usual small talk to the Job Ruse, a conversational ploy typically reserved for after-liquor-in-tiny-glasses time:

"I hope your apartment isn't much further...my hotel room is way across town, and morning comes so quickly—"

"You don't live *and* work here?" No matter where I am when they ask this question, I have to be quick on the uptake; suspicion-time, you know. Turning to smile at her (avoiding contact with her eyes), I assured her, "My job takes me from town to town...I'm an accident investigator with an insurance company. Come in, take pictures, help the bereaved file their claims—"

"So you take pictures of dead people—"

Works like a charm every time. Nothing as exciting, as secretly thrilling, as getting the chance to see some pictures of dead people—and knowing that the person showing them to you is some stranger who won't tell your friends and co-workers that you were poring over them over the dregs of coffee or liquor. I carry a couple of such pictures in my coat breast pocket (the fact that they're still slightly warm from being stored so close to my body seems to intensify the experience for the victims), just enough to whet their appetite, then tell them I have more such pictures in the trunk of my car....

And the beauty of this ruse is, it works anywhere the car can be parked, should it be necessary for me to get the whole thing over with prematurely. Capture what I can of the moment before it all dies down...

Taking one hand off the wheel, steering with my right knee and left hand, I rummaged in my breast pocket, making out for a second like they weren't there after all (*that* was because she'd made me uncomfortable, picked open a few barely-healed scabs), then triumphantly plucked them out and passed them over to her. As she snatched them out of my extended hand, I switched on the overhead light, so she could better view the glossy four-by-six snapshots of one of my car-kills. (Nobody is gullible enough to buy an accident investigation in a living room). She obviously was getting into what she saw; licking her lipsticked lips like a schoolgirl, nervously pawing at her hair, her foundation-and-powder slathered cheeks, but—best of all, to me—she began to breathe heavily, making the fabric of her tailored blouse rub exquisitely against the lace-covered surface of her slip below. Now, if she just didn't *say* anything, just let her clothes whisper and sing to me while I stopped the car and leaned over to grab my blanket-hidden ax from the foot-well behind my driver's seat—

"These are really *cool*...y'know, if there had been MTV back when we were in high school, the videos for Steely Dan's stuff would've had scenes like these in 'em—tough images, that showed you what was *really* what—"

In desperation, I shut off the CD player, just so that I could make out the sounds of her silk-on-silk clothing over the prattle of her voice; she was still yammering away, her words digging into me no matter how much I hated to even half-listen, as I floored the brake pedal, then lunged over the back seat and grabbed my ax by feel alone.

"—only, I suppose the censors would've cut the videos to ribbons...can't face the *truth* about anything—"

It was a tight squeeze, getting enough momentum with the ax in such tight quarters, but I managed to imbed the blade in the back of her head without slashing any of the car's interior in mid-swing; at the moment of impact, her eyes sort of went big, not-quite-popping out just as her mouth opened in that silent *moue* of near-surprise even the best of my victims make, and while she jerked spasmodically (who knows what psychomotor nerves I'd severed in her skull), the picture of the previous car-kill-victim fluttered out of her hand, followed shortly by the other picture she'd already put in her lap. But she didn't make any sounds; small comfort that it was, I *did* get to hear the intimate sounds her clothing made as she shifted around on the seat for that final time....

(Emphasis on the small this time around; I'd perhaps hit her too swiftly, knocking out her brain before she could do some serious thrashing around. Par for the course, I guess, given her previous upsetting performance....)

Naturally, as soon as it was over, and my ears savored the final rustle and sigh of her still-perfectly draped skirt against her silk-clad legs, I switched off the interior light, then sat next to her for a few minutes, as if I'd deliberately chosen to park here for an innocuous purpose, like smoking a cigarette. Which is what I did; not only does the sight reassure those people who might just be passing by in their cars, but it gets rid of that blood smell.

I am strictly a *sound* man...the reek of blood makes me sick.

Once I'd finished my cigarette, it was time to drive to yet another secluded, dark part of the neighborhood, then go through the after-the-kill routine; pick up the victim, put him or her (or them) on the shower curtain(s) spread out next to the car, or the open apartment door, bundle, secure, then toss the remains in the trunk of my car. How long I kept them in *there* varied; weather and my whims contribute equally to the duration. Since I wasn't in an apartment, I'd have to wash up at a service station. Put the car through a self-serve wash with the windows open, too. I had a bottle of peroxide in the trunk, next to that flash-type camera I use to take new "insurance investigator" pictures when the old ones get too blood-daubed (funny, how those one-hour photo places always buy my story about *being* a real insurance investigator).

I did pause when looking at the camera, while getting the shower curtain and the rope; my old pictures were getting a bit dog-eared. But...to record her image would've meant recording the *memory* of her—and her clothing wasn't *that* worthy of fond remembrance. No, better to forget, chalk it up to a premature... not-quite-ejaculation...of the emotional kind.

Once she was out of the car, and the peroxide was making that sizzling, *warm* sound where I'd daubed it to take up the worst of the bloodstains, I turned the CD player on again, cranking the sound to near-full blast—after I'd rolled up the windows, of course; not polite to wake up the neighborhood after a kill—and pulled away from the curb, in search of the nearest self-serve car wash. Just like that split skirt of hers...not that she still in a condition to appreciate the irony.

But I was...and like the man who sings the song says, I could always go back and do it again...just because this time things went wrong, didn't mean I might not get it right the next time.

Maybe the victim wouldn't talk over the music of his/her/their clothing—

Maybe the song would just keep on coming, taking me—and the hurt—away with it—

Maybe I wouldn't need to fast-forward to the final movement of the song, the dripping crescendo of blood before the silence.

Yeah, right, *maybe*.

In the meantime, just do it again....

AFTERWORD

Late in the 1980s, and into the early 1990s, the Canadian sketch comedy troupe The Kids in the Hall used to appear on first HBO, then Comedy Central, and finally late night weekly airings on CBS, before they pulled the plug on their self-titled show—for those readers who have yet to see them, all I'll say is that their stuff is on DVD, and by all means buy or rent or stream it if you can, and 1) if you were into Monty Python, and 2) think the majority of the stuff on SNL was somewhat over-rated, you will definitely love what you see. More subtle than most of Monty Python, and with female characters who were just that, actual characters vs. MP's caricatures of women, and far better-written for the most part than SNL, The Kids... were perhaps the funniest thing I've ever seen on TV in decades. When they stopped showing re-runs of them on Comedy Central, I was in mourning.

Among the many recurring characters the five-man troupe brought to life was an un-named fellow played by (and I assume written by) Dave Foley, who later starred in NBC's "News Radio" and voiced the part of the lead ant Flick in Pixar's *A Bug's Life*, along with numerous other TV and movie roles since The Kids... broke up—this character was an ax murderer, but not just *any* serial killer. Remarkably cheerful, articulate, neatly-groomed and incongruously innocent-looking, this fellow appeared in at least three skits/monologues that I've seen (I never saw the uncut episodes on HBO, so there may have been more appearances from him), including a witty solo scene revolving about how he'd been spending the last few years axing people to death, while all his high school classmates had pursued other career paths, and two scenes involving his post-murder interactions with a knife grinder (gotta sharpen that ax!), and an old woman who answers a knock on her door one night to find the cheerful ax murderer outside, wanting to know if he can borrow an ax, since his broke in the middle of his efforts to slaughter her neighbors. You have to see these skits to appreciate their indescribable sheer funniness; just thinking about them makes me laugh out loud.

Anyhow, in 1993, I was reading a copy of *Premiere* magazine, and came across Joseph Stefano's comment about serial killers (which opens this story)—somehow, when I read those words, they immediately merged with Mr. Foley's Cheerful Ax Murderer character, and this story came to mind virtually all of a piece. When I wrote it, I had a little "inspired by" mention of the Kids... character and Mr. Foley at the end, but somehow it was lost by the time this was finally published nearly a decade later. Bad photocopy, didn't make it into the final typeset, who knows what happened, but...hopefully better late than never, here's my acknowledgement of who actually inspired this story. Sorry it took another decade to correct the error, Dave....

THE REALTOR

Did you ever notice how the ink in a felt-tip pen tends to bleed a little at the edges when you write with one on newsprint? The way the color branches off in tiny capillary-like angles from the initial stroke of the pen? So much like rivulets of blood streaming away from that first deep slice in flesh—especially when the seeping fluids catch and hold in the fine thin colorless hairs surrounding her make-up-covered flesh, so that you can never quite tell where or how the blood will dribble out, or just what sort of crimson filigree will adhere to her cooling skin once it dries.

Maybe you don't notice stuff like that, but I do. Especially in that edgy time *before*; before I leave the last town, and select a new one (and always, I need to find a town or city big enough to support at least one large Realty company, the kind that runs those half- or full-page newspaper advertisements which show photographs of their star Realtors); before I find just the right Realtor's picture (she always has to be fairly young, passably good-looking, and preferably the kind of up-and-coming Realtor who'd be willing to cut her fellow Realtor's throats by showing a house not assigned directly to her); before I begin circling her grey-screen image with ever-widening swipes of my red-tipped pen (which always tends to create a hazy, sharp-spiked nimbus around her head and shoulders, like a crown of rusted barbed wire)—and especially before I make that call to her Realty company, and force my voice into a semblance of calm disinterest when I ask if she might be in the office that afternoon (it's always good to sound as unmemorable and neutral as possible, least some receptionist later recall my over-eager tones, or that tinge of anxious anticipation for more than a simple house showing).

As I dialed the number of the latest Realtor, in the latest new town, I watched the deep red ink seep slowly into the surrounding coarse-grained newsprint. By the time the angular spikes of crimson touched the top-most curls on her well-coifed head, the receptionist came on-line, her voice as discreetly neutral as my own.

"—Realty, may I help you?"

Forcing myself to glance away from that still-spreading nimbus of feathery red, I felt my lips form the syllables of my latest victim-to-be's name, even as I imagined what I'd be feeling as my lips ran down and around her warm, yet fear-stiffened flesh, during the time *before* I slit her throat, and watched the blood-show afterward.

"She's on another line right now, but I'll put you on hold—she shouldn't be more than a minute or two." That neutral, anonymous voice was replaced with equally neutral, anonymous instrumental music; as I clutched the receiver (the old-fashioned, thin-waisted kind, with the swelling protrusions of the ear-and-mouth pieces jutting out from either end, so much like the breasts and hips of a nude woman...a sandy beige slick-fleshed woman) tightly against my left ear, my right index finger slowly circled the red-stained newsprint surrounding her face, until the tip of my finger was stained ruddy pink. Turning my hand palm-up for a second, I realized that my fingertip looked vaguely clitoris-like in the late afternoon sunlight which filtered through my motel-room blinds.

But when I sucked on the fingertip, circled it with the tip of my tongue, it just wasn't the same...close, but the faint scent of the ink was too harsh, too astringent.

Some of my victims had gone overboard on the douche, or the feminine hygiene spray, but that only left them smelling like air-fresheners, or those fiber-board trees you hang from a rear-view mirror—and usually their own musk mingled in with the applied odors. But none of them ever smelled like marker ink—

"Good afternoon, this is—" the voice of my would-be victim broke into my reverie, instantly dispelling my olfactory mementoes to that part of my mind I privately labeled "Tracks"; her accent was just Midwestern enough to make it clear that she was a native of this area, but not too harsh or fast—but later, just before I'd shove the gag between her lips (full lips, according to her picture) her voice would be fast and harsh, as she'd plead for me not to do all the things I'd promise to do to her (in full, excruciating detail, of course, right down to how I'd watch the blood dry on her flesh afterwards—by then she'd be tied up), I knew that her carefully modulated accent would erupt in a nasal, mule-harsh bray of fear and disbelief, even as I'd unroll a snicking length of duct tape from the roll I always carry with me, and seal that under-panties gag behind her lips.

Some of my other victims were louder than mules, in fact.

But right *now*, as she sat wearing her Realty-company-supplied blazer (everyone in the advertisement's twelve photos wore the same slightly out-of-style jacket—maroon jackets, according to the copy elsewhere in the ad) in her probably-a-cubbyhole office, her flesh was free of my saliva, and her limbs were free of the silvery twists and coils of duct tape I'd wrap around them once I'd punched her into semi-unconsciousness. Her head wasn't even circled by my inked crown of prickly wood-pulp crimson.

But they soon would be.

Holding back the excitement I felt rushing and bubbling through me, that surge of anticipation which soon drifted down my torso, and made my penis jut up and out across my belly, like an eagerly-pointing finger, I smoothly launched into my usual spiel—the one that differed only in slight detail (my current name, the address of the house I'd selected, the exact time of the appointment I desired), and just as my soon-to-be victim almost always did, she cut in apologetically:

"Oh, I'm sorry, that listing belongs to another agent...I can connect you to..."

"Are you sure you couldn't show me that property? According to your company's advertisement, you're the 'Salesperson of the Month'—surely, someone in your position could bend the rules just a bit, no?"

Easing down in my chair, to better give my blood-engorged penis more room to expand in my trousers, I half-closed my eyes and began to take in motel-room-antiseptic-scented air in short, tight gasps, as she sighed softly into the phone while mulling over my request.

And while she decided, I remembered what the property I'd chosen that morning looked like—no doubt she was thinking that anyone who actually wanted to see this house had to be interested enough in it to make a serious offer.

That it was actually on a dead-end road (at the tip of that dead-end) was an unexpected plus for me; aside from that, the house met all of my typical criteria; one story plus basement, windows and doors intact (screams tend to carry through broken panes), no furniture inside, no phone service, situated toward the center of its lot instead of closely abutting another house, and the Realtor's metal sign out from was scabrous enough to indicate that this was a really old listing, one the company would want cleared from their other holdings. The hydrangea bushes in front of the downstairs front windows were a pink-blossoming gift from the gods of death, blood and exquisite pleasure—they'd better shield whatever struggle would occur once she and I were inside the property.

I'd actually walked up to the front porch (warped, graying boards which met a screen door whose screen had rusted brown tears on the surrounding once-white wood), and taken a peek inside the partially-shaded windows and window-inset front door (four rust-mottled thumb-tacks held down the remaining corners of some long-ago torn-off paper note, probably a home-drawn "For Sale" sign), just to make sure that this house really was as perfect as it seemed for my purposes.

And as far as I could tell by peering through that age-mottled dirty glass, it was—

"Well, Mr. Kern, I suppose I *could* go ahead and show you that house—you're sure that *that's* the house you'd be most interested in—"

"Oh, definitely," I lied, as I began to gently rub the heel of my free hand against the stiffening ridge beneath my trousers. "That house is everything I could ever want—there are so many possibilities there."

"Possibilities," she echoed, her voice suddenly wistful, as if she was already figuring out how to spend her almost certain commission; that barely-voiced longing made me arch up my pelvis as I bore down harder against my fabric-sheathed boner, as I thought, Babe, you don't know the meaning of the word "possibilities."

At least not until after I'd shown her what was really possible.

* * * * * * *

I had to force myself not to keep rubbing and massaging my throbbing member as I stood waiting for her outside of the house; while I'd have all evening to do with her what I wished, I didn't want to shoot the whole wad in my underwear before I so much as had a chance to touch or taste her—even though I knew I'd killed her, I didn't want to risk seeing the glint of satisfaction in her eyes as she stared at my limp, unresponsive dick. When I wasn't tensing my thighs, I was glancing at my watch; for a "Salesperson of the Month," she wasn't overly punctual. And I couldn't even see my car (I'd parked it—as was my habit—a few blocks away), so the nagging half-worry that someone might be messing with my wheels began to gnaw at me, dulling the keen edge of anticipation I *needed* before a showing. The same edge that put a spring in my step, and the surge of adrenalin behind my first well-placed blow to the back of her head once we'd actually entered the house.

Around me, the afternoon shadows began to thicken, growing deeper grey as they pooled, then seeped silently before the house, the dulling smear of darkness reaching quietly and quickly for the curb beyond the unkempt lawn of sun-baked grass—then, as my eyes reached the crumbling concrete swell of the curb, I saw the approaching car, its front doors emblazoned with the logo of my victim's Realty company. I could barely make out her face and shoulders through the windshield, but what I could see was enough to disappoint me—her hair-do seemed to be the same, but then again, these Midwestern types tended to keep the same hairstyle year after year—for it was obvious from the heaviness of her jaw-line that the picture featured in the news-paper was taken years earlier.

And when she emerged from the car, her maroon blazer pulled tightly over her ample bosom, I amended that earlier impression of when her photograph must've been taken—make that decades ago.

True, the rest of her body didn't look too bad—fair waist indentation, thick but acceptable hips, good legs that nonethe-less lacked real ankles—but it had obviously taken this woman a long, long time to work her way up the Realty ladder. But still, under that A-line skirt was her deep, soft, scented place, and under that boxy blazer her breasts had to be squishily-soft and puckered around the nipples, so this wouldn't be a total waste of my planning and anticipating—not a total success, but the sun did seem to be cooperating nicely by hiding behind a scud of clouds.

"You didn't walk all the way here, did you Mr. Kern?" Her voice still seemed youngish, but didn't I detect just the slightest hint of brassy loudness, and a slight speeding up of her words? I didn't have time to reflect on the differences between her phone voice and her actual voice, so I entered the next stage of my ruse by saying, "My car's in the shop, so I took a cab here. He said he'd come back in an hour, but—"

"Oh, no need for that. I can give you a lift into town, or to your house, whatever you prefer," At least her teeth were good; square, slightly off-white, and clean-smelling—my tongue would encounter no partially masticated hunks of her lunch while roaming around in there, while she was still unconscious enough not to try and bite it off.

"Could you? I'd much appreciate it," I replied, as I walked slowly toward the screen door, keeping pace with her own high-heeled mincing steps. Her feet were puffy enough to ooze out of the tops of her pumps, but once she was stripped, that wouldn't be so awful to look at anymore. I've never really been into feet anyhow.

I gallantly held open the screen door for her as she fumbled in her purse for the house-keys, then offered to let her into the house once she'd opened the lock, but after that, things didn't go according to my usual plan—she may've taken her sweet time mounting the steps to the porch, but once she was over the threshold, she might've been wearing running shoes instead of those patent-leather pumps. All I got was a whiff of her cologne as she breezed past me; a harsh musk, with unexpectedly heavy, astringent undertones.

Not unlike the smell of soft-tip pen ink, actually.

The odor of her cologne was strange enough to make me stand dumbfounded for a moment—and in said moment, she moved deeper into the shadowed depths of the house, down the short narrow hallway and into one of the many rooms which branched out at unexpected angles from that brief length of an entryway. Sorting out a maze-like grouping of unfamiliar rooms had never been much of a problem for me before; with only one previous exception, I'd been able to render the victim helpless within one minute of entering the latest house (and in the case of the one who dodged the first poorly-aimed blow, I managed to drag her by a fistful of her hair from the room she'd scooted into, while I bounced the back of her skull against the hardwood floor with each step I took).

Unlike the house where I'd killed the one who tried to run, this place was carpeted, musty dull green once-patterned synthetic crap that was well-padded enough to make each step a shifting, roiling one...and effectively muffle the sound of her footfalls. All I could do was try to follow the musky wake of her cologne, for the odd arrangement of the rooms (which, considering that I didn't see her move from room to room via the hallway, must've led one into the other) created weird echoes as she spoke to me:

"As you can see, this house was built after the Second World War...bedrooms are on the small side...room for an apartment-size 'fridge in the kitchen...non-grounded wiring, if you'll notice the outlet holes—"

Her muted voice was a steady, droning babble which seemed to surround me—not only from all sides, but from above and below me, too. Sort of like the way screams bounce and ricochet off concrete basement walls, only not as sharp and metallic-sounding. No heat, no fear, just that cocoon of noise filtering into my consciousness, adding to the disorienting semi-haze of coming darkness which turned the interior of the empty house into shadow-box squares, one disconcertingly like the other in their *faux*-paneled monotony.

And despite the fact that she certainly couldn't see me, she still spoke to me, giving her spiel in that barely-Midwestern voice of hers, while I tried to track her like a spoor-sniffing dog, even as the mildew-tinged dust from the carpet masked her musky trail.

For a small post-war bungalow, the place seemed to have an endless number of rooms—or very few virtually identical rooms.

As I searched for her, my penis straining at my fly like a hunting dog's out-stretched paw, I tried to ignore what she was saying, while honing in on her voice alone, hoping to catch a louder, clearer sound, but the deepening shadows somehow made it more difficult for me to hear clearly (and as I said before, that carpeting muffled both her steps and mine), so I was soon entangled in gauzy webs of distorted sound and hazy darkness, unable to even tell left from right any longer, let alone east from west—for outside those half-pulled shades, the sun had fully set, rendering me without a sense of direction, a sense of *self*—

A different sound broke through the muffled jumble; the sharp, wooden *whump*! of an opened door hitting a not-too-distant wall. Then, the unmistakable sound of clacky shoe-soles tapping down uncarpeted basement stairs. Wooden stairs, by the sound of them.

Each sharp rap of her shoe-soles hitting the treads snipped away that murking binding of darkness and echoing noise which had ensnared me; pausing just a second to snort out the cloying odor of un-vacuumed carpeting from my nostrils, I hurried in the direction of that sharp descending sound (oddly, I hadn't noticed the small sink in the kitchen before, even though I had to have entered that empty paneled room during my earlier go-'rounds, when I'd missed seeing the then-closed basement door), now guided in part by the sallow wedge of light shining from the partially-closed basement door. Just as I reached the doorway, the sound of her footfalls changed; now they rang with a cold concrete reverberation, as she made her way (still babbling to the air) across the basement floor, toward some distant spot in that clammy shell of crushed and molded stone. Probably the furnace. Or the water heater.

As I descended that unpainted wooded staircase, her voice grew louder (but not quite as loud as her screams would be once I'd torn off her ugly, unisex company blazer, sensible A-line skirt and whatever catalogue-outlet underwear she surely must be wearing—and then began to incise the outlines of her under-garments on her unadorned flesh), but the bare hanging bulb positioned in the middle of the heat-duct and electrical wire criss-crossed ceiling revealed no richly-curved silhouette of her waiting body conveniently cast on a mildew-mottled grey wall. The echo of her voice was different down here; sharper, with a granite harshness that made my ears ring, but I did make out one sentence: "I thought you'd never get down here"...right before I felt the stinging, bone-deep burst of blue-hot pain behind my left ear. Then, for a time, I felt, saw, and heard no more...even as her pungent musk-trail filled my nose and lungs like a flood of deadly, crushing water....

Despite the lingering ache in my head, I was acutely aware of one thing as I regained consciousness; she'd found—and used—my roll of duct tape while I'd been out.

Each small movement I tried to make pulled on the short hairs of my arms and legs; tiny, angry nips of pain that soon taught me to remain still. Once I stopped struggling, I felt the seeping gritty chill of the basement floor under my bare flesh—from the point where my trimmed hair met my neck to the bottoms of my ankles, all I could feel was concrete. Hard, unyielding, and just slightly damp.

Keeping my eyes closed, I tried for a moment to extract a second of pleasure from my situation (pretend you're the victim, imagine how you'd look to yourself—nipples like cold raisins, pale skin rippling with dimples and goose-pimples, matted hair covering the musky, wet place), but I was just too cold, too much in pain, to enjoy the fact that I was hog-tied and helpless in the basement of an empty house. Then a short, sharp leathery nudge in my ribcage, and her voice, now soft enough not to reverberate:

"Did I do what you would've done to me by now? Or do you prefer 'em spread-eagled?"

Even her voice seemed different now; that her scent seemed harsher, stronger, could've come from the effort she'd expended to hit, strip, then bind me, but why would her voice be deeper, stronger?

Reluctantly, I opened my eyes, and was momentarily grateful that she'd unscrewed all the downstairs hanging bulbs but one—and that remaining lit bulb was in the far end of the basement, away from the stairs, and behind the cylindrical bulk of the water heater. I don't think I could've taken a brightly-lit room, not with the thumping ache in my head.

But my eyes still opened wide when I saw her before me; even in the poor light, she was an astonishing sight—fully naked, her hair less curly, more tussled, she stood slightly off to one side, legs parted just enough to show a hint of her unparted labia under the tangle of still-matted brown curls, her arms positioned loosely akimbo on her fleshy waist, her full breasts jutting out from her sturdy ribcage just far enough to partially obscure her lower jaw and mouth. Kicking off her other shoe, so that I was now nudged with a clammy bare toe, she asked again, "Is this what you'd have done to me? Or do you like to do it standing up?"

Shaking my head *no*, fearful that sitting up or standing would only make the pain worse, I tried to look into her shadowed eyes (women don't trust men who stare at their tits while talking to them) as I gasped, "I wouldn't have done anything...not to you—"

Her breasts jiggling as she gave my hip a short, hard kick, she spat out, "Liar. Your first mistake was mentioning that cab... there's no taxi service in this town. Second mistake was being so insistent on *me* showing you *this* house. I didn't get to be "Salesperson of the Month" showing dogs like this one."

"I think you've got your mistakes in the wrong order," I said, trying to make light of the situation...as if by jollying her up, she'd think better of me, maybe let me go, or just turn me over to the cops—but the second kick on the hip gave me her answer.

Hunkering down next to me, with her bent legs parted wide enough now for me to get a shadowy glimpse of her gaping vagina beyond her wrinkled labia, she picked up the much-diminished roll of duct tape from the basement floor and began to pull off a length just long enough to cover my mouth from ear to ear.

"Do you like to gag 'em before or after fucking them?" She ripped off the free length of silvery tape and stuck it on the underside of her left forearm, then began to unpeel another bit of the tape, doing it slowly so as to increase the sticky, yielding sound of it.

Wiggling in place before her, I began to curl my knees toward my groin (my penis was now soft, limp and embarrassingly small from fear, while my balls had all but burrowed into my pelvis), as I said softly, "You've got it all wrong...I never intended to—"

"I could put this piece of tape over your nostrils, I suppose... let you gasp for air like a fish with your mouth flapping...but

I'd much rather hear what you planned to do to me." She put the newly-ripped-free piece of tape on her other forearm, before setting the roll back on the floor.

She could've put those two lengths of duct tape anywhere she chose; I knew it, and she knew it. My mouth, my eyes, my nose, anyplace that would cause the most fear and/or pain. And I already knew how much the adhering tape could pull on hair—she seemed to know it too, as she glanced at my sparse nest of closely-trimmed pubic hair, so I decided to cooperate...at least until I could worm a hand out of the bindings around my wrists, once she was close enough to grab in a choke-hold.

Settling down against the slimy coolness of the floor, I began, "First thing, I would've knocked you out within a foot of the door...like you did to me. Then, either drag you to the most out-of-the-way bedroom, or down to a place like this. Still clothed. I don't like to see skid marks on my women." She didn't laugh at my little private joke.

"Then...while you'd still be out, I'd tear off your clothes; material makes a wonderful rending sound when you tear it along the grain..." for a moment, I paused, as I relived past conquests, and once again heard those delicious sounds, "...but underwear doesn't tear so well, so that I sometimes slice it off... but it's funny, most women have those tan lines, in the shape of a bra and panties, so I accentuate those...little teasing slices, just deep enough to draw a bead of blood...ever notice, how drying blood looks lacy on flesh?" From the look in her eyes, I didn't think she'd considered it before.

"By the time I'm down to the underwear, you'd be coming to, but I'd have taped your wrists and ankles—not spread-eagle, either, but loose enough to squeeze myself in—so you couldn't do much more than scream before I balled up your panties and shoved them in your mouth. Give you a taste of yourself, so to speak...then I'd tape your mouth. But it's funny, some of them still make muffled sounds...especially when my tongue tickles their flesh, or when I shove it in...one of them spit out the gag just as I slit her throat. No matter how much I try to follow the same pattern, little things like that still happen to catch me off guard."

"So you never force them to suck you?" Her voice was curiously detached, and subtly disinterested...which somehow hurt more than the whack against my head, or resting on cold rock-hard concrete did.

"Too risky...the human jaw can exert a lot of pressure y'know. Oh, I've Frenched some of them while they're out, but it's risky, too...by the way, when I said I bind their legs loose enough, I didn't mean just for my dick—"

By now the rush of memories and sensory mementoes was having a most therapeutic effect on that same formerly soft and limp part of me; I felt a liquid, spreading warmth begin to radiate inward from my groin to my penis, and as it rose and thickened in that clammy basement air, I felt waves of pleasure ripple throughout my torso and upper thighs, as my own breaths became shorter and sharper—and soon, I felt a moist warmth outside my member, accompanied by twin puffs of soft hot breath just above my pubic bone. Glancing over at her as she bent over me, I decided to keep talking, to better distract her while I tried to work my hands free of the tape:

"It's funny...how they go from squirming against their bonds to squirming with pleasure...even after I stop tonguing them, and begin whispering what *else* I'm going to do to them as I bang them...their lips keep on twitching and jerking, even as I describe...how their blood will spurt out, then dribble over their necks and collarbones...although they begin to fight as I tell them how lacy the dried blood looks against cold flesh."

It was difficult to speak, for her tongue was a pliant, probing presence which alternately teased then assaulted my penis, while her gently kneading teeth pulled then released my blood-engorged flesh, and as she sucked, her fingers simultaneously massaged my balls and circled each of my nipples in turn, until I no longer tried to wiggle free of the tape which bound my wrists; no one had ever tongued me so violently, so desperately, but even as the first throbbing ripples of an orgasm began to race through my over body, I felt no urge to *come*...for her insistent, almost painfully expert tongue seemed to probe into my penis, as if she could somehow curl it so tightly-thin as to work that soft moistness *into* me—

It was then that I realized that her nose was now touching my pubic hairs, which just couldn't *be*—I was over seven inches when erect, yet I didn't feel the back of her mouth or the top of her throat, just that silky-yet-wet-sandpapery surface of her tongue...but as I tried to process that bit of sensory information in my aching, confused brain, another can't-be-but-it-is sensation came clear to me; the fingers which had been rubbing my balls were now rubbing a thinner layer of flesh which hugged *bone*, while the fingers of her other hand seemed to hover higher above my chest, so high that her tape-slick forearm no longer rested on my ribcage—

When I finally came, there was no hot jetting spurt of semen splashing against her palate, only an oily slick stickiness which welled within me...before her probing, burrowing tongue licked it away, leaving my tender, wrinkled exposed openness vulnerable to the room's chilly coolness.

And that same cool air now encircled my breasts...which jutted high above my ribcage, so high I could barely see beyond them as I tried to see what had happened to my penis and balls... but, if I shifted my head and looked *between* those wrinkled-flesh-tipped pale mounds of flesh, I could just make out the flattened curly mass of pubic hair in the center of my groin.

But there was nothing protruding from my hair anymore.

Not even a worm-floppy length of sated flesh, not even two sagging balls in the scrotum that was no longer there...arcing my head and shoulders up, so that I could bend slightly at the waist, I *could* make out the moist pink sheen of the upper end of labial folds—

Letting my upper body fall backwards, I winced as my injured skull impacted on the concrete; blinking the tears out of my eyes, I turned my head slightly to look at the Realtor, who now sat cross-legged off to one side, with one hand cupped under a vaguely dark-shadowed chin...while the other hand aimlessly stroked a softly wrinkled penis which jutted out limply from the tangled nest of light brown pubic curls.

"Was it good for you this time...as good as all the other times?" The voice which uttered that teasing question was mellow in its resonant softness, the syllables now as rich and warm as the cologne of sweat and musk which hung in the air between us. I was only able to take short, envious glances at the Realtor's well-defined musculature, and swept-off-the-forehead wavy hair which ended well above the shoulders, even as I couldn't help but make panicked, disbelieving visual sweeps of my own altered torso.

Pulling one length of tape off the inside of a tautly muscled forearm, the Realtor placed it over my nest of pubic hair, pressed it down with a blunt-tipped forefinger—then quickly ripped it of my pelvis, taking up a layer of curls with it.

Biting my lips against the searing pain, I finally gasped, "It was good...it was *good*...please, let me *go*...never agai...won't ever do it—" while shutting my eyes in horror.

Another snick of pulled-up tape, then the pressure was applied over my mouth before I had the chance to re-open my pressed-shut eyelids. This time, the tape stayed put, even as I tried to work my tongue between my stuck-together lips, while the Realtor shifted position, finally settling down in a semi-reclining position next to me, so that we were face to face. Smiling at me, the Realtor reached over to gently circle my still-erect nipples with a lazy forefinger, while saying, "Oh, I'm sure it was good...always was for me, anyway. But I can't let you go. Not that I disbelieve you when you say you'd never do it again... but you didn't let the others go, did you? It was good with you, but that still doesn't make you better than all the other women, does it?" before giving my left nipple a sharp hard tweak for emphasis.

I tried to reason with the Realtor behind the tape, but my words (curiously high-pitched, even when heard *through* the distortion of my own head) made no difference; giving the other nipple, then my labia, a similar deep pinch, the Realtor droned on in that husky-warm voice, "don't be so scared...I won't kill you...but I will tell you what's going to happen to you, later on.

"Remember when I said you'd made two mistakes before? Well, you made another one. Did you happen to see those four thumbtacks stuck in the front door, just under the window? Good. It's really too bad you came to this town when you did... couple of weeks ago, we had a bad thunderstorm...high winds, kind that rip notices off doors...notices like 'This Property Condemned'."

Under the tape, my lips tried to form the word *No*, but the Realtor only smiled before continuing, "And there was a date on the notice, for when the county demolition crew was supposed to come out early in the morning to tear the place down. First they step in to see if anyone's inside, but they're only getting straight time pay, so they don't waste too much time looking. The house is obviously locked anyway...then they set the dynamite charges, before using the wrecking ball on what's left. Whole thing takes less time than it would for me to actually slit your throat and watch the blood dry."

Writhing on the floor, arcing my back and my knees, I shook my head *No*, NO as the Realtor finally got up, dusted off the clinging bits of grit and dirt from his legs and buttocks with his broad, blunt-fingered hands, then padded over to the pile of clothing about ten feet from where I was trussed up on the unyielding concrete. After the Realtor put on my trousers, shirt, and shoes, then topped that off with the maroon unisex blazer, he turned to me and said, "Did you ever notice how concrete doesn't just break into big hunks after it's blown up, but sort of disintegrates into grains of sandy material around the blown-apart sections? If you're still conscious when it happens, you might want to check it out."

The Realtor walked out of sight as he spoke, but just before he mounted the steps leading to the kitchen, and right after he shut off the remaining light, he added, "You only have a few hours to wait before the wrecking crew arrives...I made sure you were unconscious for several hours before I woke you up.

"Just so you wouldn't have time to work your way free before they killed you. But you will have time to imagine what it'll be like when that concrete crumbles..."

* * * * * * *

Did you ever notice how footsteps on the floor above you echo loudly long after the person's left the room...or the house? So much like the beating of a doomed heart....

AFTERWORD

Not long after I wrote a short-short story based on the same basic premise as this tale ("Murder by Appointment," in a different Borgo collection), I got to thinking that I hadn't really explored all the possibilities of the basic killer-meets-Realtor-in-an-empty-house scenario...and came up with this. Once I had the twist-ending in mind, the thing pretty much wrote itself. While I also like the short, literal version of this as a mystery, I do prefer this take on the concept.

It's much nastier than many of the stories which came before it; after it was published, I received some positive feedback from male writers, who thought I handled the physical sensations of being male well, given the face that I'm female, so I guess I did something right here!

Years later, an episode of one of my favorite TV shows, CBS' *Criminal Minds*, also briefly utilized this basic killer-stalks-Realtor-in-empty-house scenario in "Limelight"—one thing I've noticed about that show in general is that their many female writers tend to come up with some of the nastiest, visceral episodes! Maybe it's just a girl thing....

ABOUT THE AUTHOR

A. R. MORLAN WAS born in Chicago, IL on January 3, 1958, and moved with her family to the Los Angeles area in 1961, where she lived until 1969, when her family moved to Wisconsin, where she still lives.

Morlan has a BS degree in English (Liberal Arts), *Magna Cum Laude* from the now defunct Mount Senario College in Ladysmith, Wisconsin, which folded shortly before a F3 tornado tore apart her town of residence in 2002. She has been a free-lance writer since 1983, and has had fiction and non-fiction published in over 130 different magazines, anthologies, collections, and e-zines in the US, Canada and parts of Europe, in addition to two novels, *The Amulet* and *Dark Journey* (both available from Borgo Press), a story collection (*Ewerton Death Trip*, Borgo Press), a Romanian-language collection called *Femia Coperta* (*Cover Woman*) which came out in 2004, a couple of upcoming collections from Borgo Press, a co-edited (with Martin H. Greenberg) anthology called *Zodiac Fantastic* (DAW, 1997), and assorted introductions for various short fiction collections by other authors. She is single and childless, but a proud pet-parent of a varying number of cat-children.

www.ingramcontent.com/pod-product-compliance
Lightning Source LLC
Chambersburg PA
CBHW050742250626
47155CB00005B/1881

* 9 7 8 1 4 3 4 4 4 4 6 7 7 *